AMBUSHED AND OUTGUNNED!

Slocum caught a faint glimpse of the gun smoke from the side of the hill. He crawled over to his dying horse and yanked the rifle from the scabbard. The bastards had bushwhacked him—and Slocum hated getting caught with his pants down. He hadn't expected Ma and her boys to try to ambush them this quickly. He cursed himself silently and fired off some shots in the direction of the gun smoke. . . .

DON'T MISS THESE
ALL-ACTION WESTERN SERIES
FROM THE BERKLEY PUBLISHING GROUP

THE GUNSMITH by J. R. Roberts
Clint Adams was a legend among lawmen, outlaws, and ladies. They called him . . . the Gunsmith.

LONGARM by Tabor Evans
The popular long-running series about U.S. Deputy Marshal Long—his life, his loves, his fight for justice.

LONE STAR by Wesley Ellis
The blazing adventures of Jessica Starbuck and the martial arts master, Ki. Over eight million copies in print.

SLOCUM by Jake Logan
Today's longest-running action western. John Slocum rides a deadly trail of hot blood and cold steel.

JAKE LOGAN

HELL TO MIDNIGHT

BERKLEY BOOKS, NEW YORK

HELL TO MIDNIGHT

A Berkley Book / published by arrangement with
the author

PRINTING HISTORY
Berkley edition / December 1993

ISBN: 0-425-14010-5

HELL TO MIDNIGHT

1

Mace Tidley had been a conductor on the Houston to Weatherford stretch of the Houston and Texas Central Railroad back in the days when the wild Comanche and Apache galloped alongside the train on defiant murder raids. A Comanche arrow had missed the tip of his nose on more than one occasion, and Tidley could still feel the hot gasp of air as if it had happened yesterday. A young Luke Short had once pointed a gun at Tidley's head. He'd also lived through catastrophic derailments and raging fires in the passenger cars. After thirty years working the rails, there wasn't too much Mace Tidley hadn't seen.

Times were civilized now, Mace knew, compared to when those bloodthirsty red savages and the merciless train robbers of years past made every journey a new adventure in fear. There hadn't been a train robbery or an Indian attack on his run in quite some time.

Which is why, when the tall, gaunt-looking, and very dirty man—the same one Tidley had eyed sus-

piciously when they'd taken him on in Oakwood—
stood and fired a shot up into the air that left a
sizable hole in the roof of the car, Tidley was surprised indeed. Tidley was in the middle of punching
a ticket, and looked up suddenly.

"This here's a robbery," the tall man announced.
The dozen or so passengers—church ladies, well-
dressed merchants, kids here and there with their
mothers—all gasped audibly. A few screams pierced
the steady, loud clanking of the wheels. In the rear
seat sat two painted ladies who'd been run out of
Oakwood and were headed to Laredo or maybe El
Paso to ply their carnal trade. The ladies of the
night were the only ones who didn't look scared.
Tidley knew they had probably both been underneath worse brutes.

The tall man approached Tidley, who finally got a
good look at him close up. He'd seen that ugly leer
plastered on more than a few wanted posters. With
some horror, Mace Tidley realized he was staring at
the most dreaded member of the Ma Fisher gang—
her oldest and kill-craziest son, Bo.

Without being told, Tidley raised his arms above
his head.

"You can't rob this train alone, Bo," Tidley said,
his voice cracking. The Fishers were supposed to be
much further north, in Oklahoma Territory—or so
he'd heard.

"Don't intend to," Bo Fisher said, and shot Tidley
twice in the chest. Tidley went careening backwards
and slammed into the door of the passenger car. He
slumped to the floor, blood squirting from the holes
in his torso.

Bo fired a round or two into the passenger car.

Women screamed and children bellowed as bullets ricocheted throughout the car, sending shards of glass and wood into the air as everyone dived for cover.

Outside, two riders spurred their horses ahead of several others until they came even with the cab of the locomotive. The engineer was giving the throttle all she had as two men frantically shoveled coal into the furnace. The riders started blasting, and hit one of the shovelers, who grabbed his belly and staggered back, then fell off the locomotive. He then held one of the gunmen's reins tightly with one hand, and trained his gun on the engineer. Two well-placed shots took off a nice big chunk of the guy's head. The gunman came within a foot or two of the cab and leaped off his horse, landing flat on top of the dead engineer. He jumped to his feet as the second shoveler came at him with the tool of his trade. The gunman drew and pumped a shot into the man's face. The man dropped like a sack of lead.

The gunman grabbed the brake and brought the train to an earsplitting, screeching stop. Besides three passenger cars, there was a mail car and a caboose.

The riders—there were at least ten of them—reined their mounts opposite the passenger cars. Some sat astride their horses pointing rifles, while others dismounted and walked toward the train, guns drawn.

Inside the train, Bo Fisher was already rounding up the passengers, jerking them out of their seats and shoving them into the aisle. He herded them off the train, while two of the other riders were doing the same to the passengers in the other two cars.

Bo approached the two prostitutes and pointed his rifle at them. Neither of them seemed overly concerned, unlike the other passengers who were shrieking and crying.

"You two waitin' for a special invite?" Bo said. He was big and ugly. *Hell*, thought one of the whores, *you could throw him in a lake and skim ugly for a month.*

Bo pushed the twin barrels of his rifle into the breast of the whore on the right, a heavily made-up strawberry blonde who'd seen better days. Not even the twelve layers of paint on her face could hide the half-moon circles under her eyes, or the weariness of her spirit. The other was a brunette who bordered on pretty, though the life of a Colorado mining town crib girl had hardened her features to angry granite.

Bo toyed with the blonde, making circles around her breasts with the tip of the rifle. "You got nice big titties."

"And I'd like to keep 'em," she said coldly, barely flinching. "We're going."

She motioned to her friend to get a move on, but before the blonde could move, Bo slid the barrels up slowly from her breasts to her slender throat. "You ladies sit tight," Bo said with a toothless grin. He moved the barrels up and pressed them against the blonde's red lips.

"Take the serpent, lady," Bo hissed. The blonde reluctantly parted her lips. Bo eased the barrels into her mouth. "Close your lips around 'em and start suckin'." He jammed the double barrels a little further. The brunette gasped, looking even paler than usual.

"You do know how to suck, don't you?" Bo asked, his finger firmly against the trigger. "Just pucker your lips and take the air." His grin stretched a little wider. "Let me see you make some love to mah gun."

Her eyes, furious with rage, never left his yellow bloodshot ones. She sucked the barrels of the rifle, running her tongue over the cold metal. Bo, his expression one of dreamy, wet lust, tickled the trigger of his Winchester and started drooling. Saliva, brown from the foul tobacco he chewed, bubbled from the corner of his mouth.

Bo's younger half brother, Little Bo (their mother, exhausted after delivering yet another son, had neither the energy nor the patience to think of a new name) appeared at one end of the passenger car brandishing his rifle. He had a handkerchief over his nose and mouth. Little Bo was a scrawny young pup whose father was, like most of his brothers, of unknown origin, and probably one of the many prairie rats who had hooked up with the gang.

"What the hell you doin'?" Little Bo called out waving his rifle. "Ain't no money in her mouth, you butt hole. Get a move on."

"You shut up," the elder Bo said to his brother. "Get yer own wimmen."

"We ain't here fer that," Little Bo snapped. "You get a move on or Ah'll tell Ma."

"You go to hell," Bo said. He viewed his bastard baby brother as little more than a piece of snakeshit. "I ain't afraid of her."

"Then y'all won't care when I tell Ma you said such," Little Bo challenged.

Big Bo yanked the rifle from the whore's mouth in a rage and turned it on his half brother. "Don't get me riled, shit bird."

For two seconds they stayed deadlocked, rifles

trained on each other's hearts—brother against brother. There was little love lost between them. Having the same mother cut no ice in their cold hearts.

Little Bo looked away and surveyed his brother's new goods. Women were kind of scarce in the Fisher gang. Little Bo said, "What the hell, bring 'em along. Maybe Ma'll let us keep 'em for a spell. If nothin' else, we can sell 'em for a fair piece in Mexico."

Little Bo turned and jumped back off the train. Outside, the gang was rounding up the frightened travelers and forcing them up against the train.

"You git along now," Bo said, prodding the whores with his rifle. The two whores obeyed, jumping up and leaving the train, with Bo trailing them at gunpoint.

One of the gang, Del Center, was going up and down the line of terrorized travelers, happily waving a Colt under their noses. They deposited cash, jewelry, and gold pieces into the hat he held in his other hand.

"Thank you, sir," he said, moving from an aging gentleman to his wide-hipped, stylishly dressed missus, who dropped expensive jewelry into his hat. "Thank you, kind lady." He gave her breast a healthy squeeze.

Within a minute or two, the train robbers had rounded up the passengers and what was left of the crew: one trembling brakeman and a Negro porter who'd been asleep in the men's lavatory with a half-shined shoe in his hand.

Hank Fisher, one of Bo and Little Bo's older brothers, rode up. He was a hulking, sinister figure who seemed even larger than his six and a half feet of solid muscle, and one of the few Fisher brothers who had half a brain. Another of the brood, Mortimer Fisher, who was a year or two younger than Hank and twice as crazy, galloped up beside him. Both dismounted and handed their reins to Little Bo, who said proudly, "Got 'em all rounded up for you, Hank."

Hank grunted. Mortimer grunted, too. Together they surveyed the scene. Little Bo and their gunners seemed to have everything under control. The passengers looked suitably frightened. Hank nodded to Mortimer, who stuck two fingers in his mouth and gave a shrill whistle. The sounds of approaching hoofbeats pierced the hot, dry west Texas air and the shrieks of the terrified passengers. A cloud of dust accompanied what looked to be two riders. As they drew closer, the frightened whimpers of the women and children—and even some of the men—quieted to just a moan here and there. Expressions of stark terror, as though they'd seen Satan himself, stole across their terrified faces. Small children huddled against their parents, and one little boy attempted to hide under his mother's petticoat.

"Lord help us," one old man whispered to no one in particular as he watched the lead rider slow to a halt. This rider was broad-shouldered, and powerfully built with short thick legs like logs.

She was also an old woman.

It was a little hard to tell at first glance, given her baggy blue jeans, battered ten-gallon hat, and black leather boots. Only the sight of her sagging but substantial bosoms proved that she was a member of the fairer sex—though just barely. A mean-spirited scowl seemed permanently frozen on her face, which was not as pretty as a bucket of mud.

A scarred pouch of flesh hung down above her left eye, concealing half of it; above it was a jagged scar. The result made half of her face look lopsided and more sinister. Even from a distance, one could see the fury and madness in her soulless black eyes. A Winchester .44–90 was tucked firmly inside the scabbard of her saddle, and she sported the latest fashions from Smith & Wesson strapped around her formidable waist.

"Ma Fisher!" the old man gasped.

Behind her a second rider appeared, a tall, thin wrinkled old buzzard who was dressed like a preacher, all in black. He was wearing a floppy, black wide-rimmed hat.

"Praise Jeh-sus!" he bellowed as he reined his horse in. "The day of Revelations has done arrived!"

Four of the gang rushed to help the "lady" down, knocking each other over in the process. Mortimer Fisher, who more than matched his mother in the meanness and sadism departments, pushed through the boisterous and eager-to-please gang members, knocking them aside like rotted fence posts.

Mortimer extended his hand to his mother. "Let me help you down, Ma," he said.

Ma Fisher grabbed the saddle horn, and started to dismount. She was wide and bulky, but she was all solid. She pulled one foot from the stirrup and held out a hand to her son. Then, like lightning, she kicked him hard in the mouth with the toe of her boot, putting her back into it. Mortimer's head snapped back like a cork from a sarsaparilla bottle. It was the only part of his massive body that moved. He spit out blood and several brown teeth, never changing his expression.

"I don't need your help, peckerwood," Ma Fisher snapped, and hopped down off her horse. "Del!" she barked, seeing the half-wit with a hatful of money, jewelry, and other goodies. "Bring it here, now."

Del Center trotted dutifully up to Ma Fisher and handed her the treasure-filled hat. "Here you be, Ma," he said. She snatched it away from him, inspecting it greedily.

Del Center pushed his luck. "What's there fer me, Ma?" he asked, his ferret face crinkling in a grin that made him look like a rotting jack-o'-lantern.

"The back of me hand," Ma Fisher rasped, and gave Center just that, smacking him wide across the face and sending the scrawny outlaw reeling back into the arms of Bo Fisher. Bo heaved him away, right into brother Hank, who smashed Del twice in the face just for sport and also pushed him away. Center staggered four steps and fell to his knees, then collapsed flat on his face into the dirt.

Ma Fisher handed the hat to Mortimer and plucked a small leather whip from her side pocket. Then she strolled over to Center, who was struggling to get to his feet. She started lashing at him as though he was nothing but a runaway sow. Center tried to ward off the blows by huddling to protect his head. Ma kicked him viciously until he rolled onto his back, then she really went to work on him with the whip. The hard, seasoned leather carved crimson gashes in his face and neck. By this time, Center offered no resistance. To do so would make Ma even more riled. Best to grimace and bear it.

Ma quickly got tired of whipping Center and moved on. She surveyed the passengers. They all looked shit-eating scared and she knew they would offer no resistance. Nasty Nick Santos, one of the gang's stalwarts and a favorite of Ma's, had the brakeman by the throat with one hand, and his other hand was holding his six-shooter at the man's head. Nick was an enormous Mexican who was equally at home breaking legs as he was breaking the English language. Ma had found him ten years ago, the half-starved son of a dying prostitute, on the streets of Nuevo Laredo. "Someone to tend the horses," she told her rabid brood of five sons, youthful desperados who were instantly jealous of the young Meskin bastard. Truth was, Ma saw something in Nasty Nick—someone who could learn to be a good *pistolero* and would take orders, whether to make a pot of coffee or blow someone's head off. Her demonic maternal instinct was on the money: Nasty Nick, as she named him, grew to become totally loyal to Ma and killed for her without remorse.

Ma walked over to Nasty Nick and the brakeman, whose face was the sickly green color of a new toma-to. She pulled out a six-shooter and stuck the barrel between the brakeman's eyes.

"How many men inside the mail car?" she asked.

Sweat rolled down the little man's plump cheeks. He tried to think, but no thoughts came. Ma cocked the trigger of her gun. The brakeman started stammering.

"I . . . it's . . . I think . . ." he sputtered nervously.

"You're lying," Ma Fisher said, and squeezed the trigger. There was a explosion, and a portion of the brakeman's head suddenly disappeared in a fine spray of bone and blood. Nasty Nick relaxed his grip; the brakeman's lifeless body sagged to the ground.

"I'll see you hang," cried one of the passengers, a

well-dressed gentleman of fifty or thereabouts, with white hair and an expensive suit. He looked indignant and put-upon.

Ma Fisher turned to him, still clutching her gun. She already hated his wretched, phony upper crust guts.

"Do I know you?" Ma asked this dignified old fart.

"Morris William Thomas the Third, president of the First National Bank of Austin," the old man said angrily. "And if I do say, your behavior here is nothing short of atrocious and totally inhumane."

"Is that right?" Ma Fisher asked.

"You shot an unarmed man," Morris William Thomas the Third said, his look one of disgust. "As God is my judge, you'll all hang."

Ma Fisher pulled out her other six-shooter and hurled it at the officious banker, who barely managed to catch it.

"Now *you're* armed, Mister Fancy Pants," Ma Fisher snarled. "Let's see what you can do."

The white-haired banker studied the weapon in his hand, remembering his younger days on the wild Texas frontier fighting Mexican bandits and the Comanche. He drew on her, aiming straight for where most folks' hearts were. He squeezed the trigger once, then twice, and heard nothing but a dry click. The chamber, he realized with some horror, was empty.

Ma's sons and the rest of the gang started chuckling. Her empty gun trick never failed to bring gales of hearty laughter among them.

"You lose," Ma Fisher said, and fired three shots into the banker's belly. A chorus of screams erupted.

One woman fainted dead away and her husband went to assist her. Another one of Ma's sons, Slug, the youngest at nineteen, drew his gun and shot the woman's husband in the ass. Slug hated sudden movement.

The man howled in pain as blood gushed out through the hole in his derriere. This brought another chorus of screams from the women. Slug fired a shot into the air and cried out, "Y'all hush up now, less y'all want the same."

The skinny, hollow-cheeked man who'd ridden in with Ma rushed gleefully to the body of the dead banker, who was already drawing flies. He produced a Bible from his black frock coat. " 'An angry man stirreth up strife and a furious man aboundeth in transgression,' sayeth Proverbs, chapter fifteen, verse eighteen," the man bellowed, the wind having a tough time making its way through his greasy black hair, and his expression one of maniacal glee. "Damn not this heathen's soul, Lord," the pop-eyed parson ranted on, looking up at heaven now. "He knoweth not from shit!" The preacher waved his Bible at the other passengers, spittle erupting on his lips. "This man here," he said, motioning to the lifeless banker, "was a sinner! 'Vengeance is mine,' sayeth the Lord! 'Strike down thine enemies and smite them,' the Good Book says."

There were few who wanted to dispute the insane rantings of this lunatic. He raged, "The bowels of hell await all who do not follow the ways of our Lord, Jesus Christ! You're all sinners, every weak one of you!" He eyed the frightened passengers suspiciously. He focused in on a girl of twelve with blonde pigtails and budding young breasts. She cowered behind her mother. The preacher grabbed one of her pigtails and tore her away from her mother, who started whimpering helplessly. The preacher pocketed his Bible and pulled a Colt .45 from under his belt. He stuck the business end of it in the girl's ear. She screamed good and loud, exciting the crazed preacher even more.

"Your soul is soiled and therefore must be cleansed," he announced. "Only through the spirit of God shall ye find true salvation!"

"Preacher!" Ma Fisher snapped, as she and her sons made their way down to the mail car—the one that contained the safe and a month's payroll for the railroad employees. Ma knew that the railroad always paid their people on the last Friday of the month. The money had been sent from Houston the Wednesday before. She'd timed this one to the second. "Drop that kid and go fetch me the dy-no-mite."

The preacher protested, "But I was about to save her soul, Ma."

"Save it later, you Jesus-jumpin' asshole," Ma Fisher snapped. "Fetch me the dy-no-mite else I'll wail the tar out of yer!"

Preacher grunted and tossed the girl back into the waiting arms of her mother. He went to his saddle-bags and pulled out five sticks of TNT. "Damn you to hell, Ma Fisher," he mumbled to himself. "A heathen through and through. There's a baptism of blood awaitin' you, that's fer sure."

Ma and a few of the boys made their way down to the mail car. "Get them people back on the train and keep 'em there," she said to the rest of her gang.

"They give you any trouble, plug 'em."

They obeyed, and set to herding the cleaned-out passengers back onto the train. At that moment, Bo Fisher appeared at the end of the car escorting the two prostitutes off. He shoved them down the steps, and they flopped gracelessly into the brown dust. Ma roared with laughter, as did her sons.

"Looky what I got here, Ma," Bo said. "Some femmy-nine companionship."

"You know how I feel 'bout wimmin when we're workin'," she rasped. "All they do is make good boys bad." Ma kicked the blonde whore in the butt as she attempted to get to her feet. The whore collapsed on her face. The brunette made no effort to get up, seeing no use in it.

"Oh, come on, Ma," Bo protested. "Been forever since me'n the others had us some. You promised, next place we come to we could grab us off a piece."

"This ain't the place," Ma croaked. "This here's a job. Forget them whores and give your brothers some help."

"But you promised, Ma," Bo said, looking hurt. He'd always been one of Ma's favorites, and what little warmth she had left in her heart went out to him.

Ma looked down at the whores, whose faces were smeared with dirt.

"Make a deal with you, son," Ma said, her eyes never leaving the blonde. "You can keep one of 'em."

Bo chewed his lip nervously. "I'll take the blonde," he said.

Ma clucked her tongue and then pumped three shots into the blonde whore's face. Three gaping red holes appeared in the whore's forehead. She crumpled to a heap. Ma shot the other one next.

"Aw, Ma," Bo squawked. "That weren't fair."

"Life ain't fair, son," she said, and proceeded to the mail car, where most of the gang was already assembled and waiting for her instructions. Preacher clutched the dynamite anxiously; he loved seeing things explode.

"How many men inside?" Ma asked.

"Two," Little Bo volunteered. "One guard, one railroad geek."

"Says who?"

"Railroad detective, right before we kilt him," Little Bo said, pointing to a man's body. There was a bullet hole in the side of his head. A tarnished badge pinned to the inside of his lapel glinted in the sun.

Preacher stepped up beside Ma, offering the dynamite. His eyes were ablaze with blood lust.

"Trains are instruments of the Devil," Preacher said. "Back to purgatory is where they belong." He fondled the dynamite affectionately. "Let me blast this iron serpent back into hell!"

"Hold your water, Preacher," Ma Fisher said. She walked slowly up to the door of the mail car, taking her sweet time about it. Her sons and the rest of the gang remained stock-still. She stopped maybe ten feet from the door of the mail car and drew her Winchester rifle.

"You in there!" she barked, her voice like sandpaper against a blackboard. "This here is Ma Fisher. You know who I am?"

There was a moment of silence, then a small voice inside the mail car called out, "I heard tell of you."

"Then y'all know I'll slaughter every man, woman, and kid on this here train iffen you don't open your doors and save me the trouble of blowing you sky high."

The men inside the mail car, judging from their silence, had obviously decided that they were dead either way, and were going to make a stand for it. Ma waved her gang on, and they started to advance, guns drawn.

"I'm callin' up my boys," Ma shouted at the occupants of the mail car. "Open them doors or the buzzards'll be chowin' down on your innards."

Common sense triumphed. The left side of the car door slid open with a creak. A nervous, bespectacled face peered out, no doubt taking inventory. One look at Ma Fisher and her boys was worth a thousand words. The odds were in favor of surrendering and hoping for the best.

Preacher stepped forward and piped up, "Heed the woman's word, heathens. Ezekiel seven tells us, 'The time is come, the day draweth near, let not the buyer rejoice—' "

Ma Fisher turned and shot Preacher's hat off. Preacher grabbed the top of his head and cried, "As ye reap so shall ye sow, Ma Fisher! The day will come—"

Ma squeezed off a shot at Preacher's feet, kicking up a burst of dust an inch away from the big toe of his boot.

"You shut the hell up!" Ma barked.

"It's the gates of hell you'll be a-passin' through, Ma Fisher," Preacher cried.

"And when I do," Ma growled back at him, "it'll be your sorry ass on line ahead of me."

The moon-faced railroad clerk pushed back the door and jumped out, landing on his knees. He was a skinny old cuss and his spectacles hug comically from one ear. Behind him, a potbellied man wearing a cheap suit and a derby also jumped from the train, though not landing quite as gracefully as the old clerk had. He landed facedown in the dust. Ma Fisher and her sons started laughing, and the rest of the gang followed suit. The railroad dick looked up indignantly, spitting soil.

"Git up," Ma ordered. Both men, visibly shaken, got to their feet. Their arms went to the sky without being asked.

"Never could abide a coward," Ma said, and turned her rifle on the chubby detective. " 'Specially one what's supposed to be upholdin' the law. How dare you not earn yer pay."

She fired a shot into his right eye. The railroad dick grabbed his face and fell backwards. He twitched a few times, then lay still.

Ma Fisher turned to her gang. "Let's take her, boys!" she hollered.

Ma and her litter of prairie rats stormed the mail car, leaving Del Center and Nasty Nick to keep an eye on the passengers. Ma saw with delight there were wooden crates no doubt filled with rifles in one corner, an added bonus, she guessed. The crates were consigned to somewhere in California. As some of her boys ripped into the mailbags like hungry hyenas, Ma went right for the safe. "Blow the safe, Preacher," Ma ordered.

The man of the dirty cloth produced some dynamite and set about his task. Ma turned her attention to the crates, where her boys were already prying off the lids. Inside, to their dismay, were not rifles but some fancy framed pieces of art.

"What the hell . . . ?" Ma croaked. Two of the men pried open one of the crates with the butts of their rifles. Precious works of art spilled out onto the floor.

"It's just a bunch of ugly pitchers," Little Bo said disgustedly, picking one up off the floor and scrutinizing it. "Just some old hag sitting in a rocking chair. What the hell kind of pitcher is this?" A word was scrawled in the bottom right corner of the painting. "What's that say, Ma?"

" 'Whistler'," Ma said, then examined the portrait of the old woman in black wearing a white cap on her head. "Shit, don't look like she's whistlin' to me." She spit a stream of tobacco juice all over the art. Elsewhere, the other men were staring openmouthed at the exotic collection of framed artworks. Another was a picture of some homely dame with long dark hair sitting in a chair with her hands crossed. She had no titties to speak of. Hank Fisher commented, "Kinda homely, ain't she? Any barkeep that hangs this over his bar is a fool." There was a little white tag hanging from the painting.

"Hey, Ma," Hank called out. "What's this here say?"

Ma Fisher snorted in disgust; times like this she always paid the price for never learning her idiot sons to read and write. The only words they knew were "wanted" and "reward."

Ma was getting angrier by the second. Not only were there pictures instead of rifles, the pictures were stupid. She turned and rammed her boot through the painting, and a rainbow of colored paint chips exploded all over the place, leaving a black hole where her head had been. Ma ripped off the tag and read, " 'Mo-na Lee-sa by Dah Vin-see. On loan from the Loo-vare M-moo-see-um, Paris, France'." She threw down the worthless tag and added, looking at the hole in Mona Lisa's head, "Looks like this Lisa's moanin' right good now."

Mortimer Fisher was looking at a picture of a bunch of bulldogs dressed just like regular people, sitting around a table playing poker, smoking cigars, and drinking hooch. Mortimer scratched his head.

"I didn't know dogs could play poker," he said to his brother, Slug.

"Looks like they know how to cheat, too," Slug observed, pointing to the painting where one of the dogs had an ace of clubs tucked into the hatband of his derby.

Their attention was diverted from the art collection by the smell of burning fuses. Preacher had rigged the safe with six sticks of dynamite, where two would have more than sufficed.

"She's all set," Preacher said, shaking out a match.

Ma Fisher shrieked, "You blanket head! I tole you *one* stick of dynamite with a *six*-inch fuse!"

"I thought you said *six* sticks of dynamite with a *one*-inch fuse," Preacher said innocently.

"Maybe I'm wrong," Hank piped up as the flaring fuse sizzled a fraction of an inch closer to the dynamite, "but I reckon that stuff's about to blow."

The Fisher clan dived off the train en masse and tumbled away just as the mail car exploded with a fiery, deafening blast that sent everything a mile high. Chunks of burning wood and shredded mail rained down. The remains of the safe—a smoldering hunk of metal—crashed to the ground a few inches from Mortimer's head. The shock from the blast had sent the passengers slamming to the ground in helpless horror and spooking the horses. They started to gallop off in fright.

Unfortunately for Nails Henry, another gang member who'd been assigned to holding the horses' reins, the terrified animals took him along, dragging him through the weeds and rocks.

"Git them horses!" Ma cried, less worried about Nails Henry, who'd be more or less cut to ribbons when the horses got through with him. He was expendable.

While half the gang chased the fleeing horses, Ma got unsteadily to her feet, her ears ringing like wind chimes. Preacher, who had landed next to her, also attempted to rise. Ma buried a spur in his bony ass and Preacher howled in pain. Burning shreds of cash floated lazily to the ground. Hank Fisher pulled out his pistol and aimed at Preacher's head. "Let me drill him, Ma," Hank snorted. "The stupid bastard."

Most times Ma Fisher would have gladly agreed to her son's request, but she wanted to keep Preacher around. When he wasn't spouting biblical gibberish, he was the only member of the gang who could service Ma in a bedroll and not get sick to his stomach.

"We need him, boy," Ma snapped. "Let him be."

"You mean *you* need him," Hank spat.

Ma backhanded Hank, cracking him solidly on the jaw. "You shut your filthy mouth." Her eyes were cold black dots. Mother or not, he was only too aware that she'd cut him from neck to nuts if he dared back talk her. He wisely let it pass.

"We sure did make a mess here," Mortimer said, indicating the dead and the wounded. "Law will be on us like beans on rice fer sure."

"We best head down to Mexico a little ahead of schedule," Slug said.

"The hell with that," Ma said. "We're goin' to Mexico all right, but we got to make this trip profitable one way or t'other. Who's got that map?"

Little Bo produced the map, and Ma had a quick look. "There's Walnut Springs to the southeast, 'bout forty miles," she said.

"Nothin' but a few bars and a church," Hank said, then pointed to a second town forty or so miles to the southwest—a two-day ride that lay directly in the path of Nuevo Laredo and the deserts beyond.

"Roseville," Mortimer said, pointing to the small burg on the map. "Word is, there's some real money to be made there—and it's smack dab in the middle of our path."

"Sounds good, Ma," Little Bo said. " 'Specially now. Them Pinkertons'll be on us now like flies to a shit house."

"We'll be in Mexico long before those skunks catch us," Ma said. She turned to her youngest son. "Slug, take Del and Nasty Nick with you and ride into Roseville. Get the lay of the land—how much law they got, how big's the bank—stuff like that."

"Where do I find you?" Slug asked. "Gonna hole up somewhere?"

"Been years since I been in these parts," Ma said, "but if I recollect right, used to be a small ranch owned by Cy Roberts. Rode with him back in fifty-one. Cy's prob'ly long dead, but odds are good the ranch is still there. It's about thirty miles due south-west. We'll wait for you there."

Slug nodded and went to round up Nasty Nick and Del Center. As he walked off, Ma yelled to him, "If ye don't show up in three days, I'll figger there's trouble and we'll come in after ye."

Slug turned and grinned, then replied, "Ain't no shit hole of a town—'specially one named *Rose*ville—kin hurt me."

"Bah," Ma Fisher croaked. "Can't recall fer sure who yer daddy was, but if I let him shoot his seed between my loins, he was two times the man you'll ever be."

Mortimer scratched his head and asked, "That mean he had to shoot his seed twice't?"

"Blasphemy!" Preacher ranted, and brandished his Bible, waving it in the air. He was still lying on the ground smarting from Ma Fisher's spur, but when the spirit moved him, he liked to share it with the world. "Heed the call of the Good Book and speak not of lust and sin! Repent now, for—"

"Shut up, fool." Ma fired a shot that nicked the edge of the Good Book and sent it flying out of Preacher's hand. "You want to keep breathin', you best start spewin' some prayers for my boy, Slug, who's ridin' into danger and then some." She cocked her pistol and aimed at Preacher's face.

"Blessed is the man that trusteth in the Lord," Preacher said dutifully, scrambling in the dirt for his Bible. "Jeremiah seventeen tells us, 'For he shall be as a tree planteth by the waters, and that spreadeth—' "

"That's enough," Ma snapped, and said to Slug, who for some unexplained reason was her favorite among the passel of rattlesnakes she'd produced, "You watch yer ass, boy." Her tone was that of someone who could almost pass for human.

"I'll watch it, Ma," Slug said.

2

Roseville, Texas. Slocum had seen worse.

A mercantile, a hotel, four saloons, a church, livery, and a lot of dust. Not unlike dozens of west Texas towns. Slocum rode in leisurely down the main street, in no particular hurry. After four days on the trail, what he wanted most was a hot bath, a shave, and a steak dinner. A pretty woman wouldn't be bad either—or maybe even one who wasn't pretty, as long as she was available. In each saloon he passed a bottle of whiskey called his name.

First things first, he decided. He was down to his last fifty, enough for either two months of easy living, or two days of raising hell. Of course, he didn't raise nearly as much hell as he used to; these days, the thought of clean sheets excited him almost as much as a wild night in town.

He rode on until he reached the jail. The shingle hanging on the door read "Chester Perkey, Marshal." It looked slightly weathered; a good sign. It meant Perkey had been around a while. There might even be some semblance of law and order in Roseville,

Slocum decided as he mounted the steps. Even better, the jail was solid brick, one of the sturdiest buildings in town. He dismounted and tied his roan to the hitching post.

He would check his guns with Perkey out of courtesy, then see about any bounties that needed hunting. Once inside though, there was no Chester Perkey to be found, only a little boy of about seven or eight in faded overalls gripping the thick bars of a jail cell. The kid had hair the color of straw and enough freckles to cover the moon.

"Where's the marshal?" Slocum asked the boy.

"Down to the hotel havin' his dinner," the kid said.

"Thanks." Slocum turned to leave. He suddenly turned back and said to the youth, "What's your name, boy?"

"Alfred Babcock," the boy said.

"How old are you, Alfred?" Slocum asked.

"Eight and a half."

"What're you in for?"

"Stealing an apple pie off'n Missus Swayzee's windowsill," Alfred said. "Pa says pie stealing is almost as bad as horse stealing."

"Your pa's right as rain," Slocum said. "How long you in for?"

" 'Til supper time," Alfred said. "Who are you?"

"Name's John Slocum."

"Really?" The kid got all excited. "John *Slocum!*"

"Heard of me?"

"No," Alfred said innocently, and eyed Slocum's gun belt. "Bet you couldn't hit a chorus line of fat ladies."

"And how would you be knowing about a chorus

line of fat ladies?" Slocum wanted to know.

Alfred gripped the bars a little tighter and tried to look tough, stiffening a bit. "I get around," he said.

"I bet you do," Slocum said dryly. He went for the door, and added, "Just don't try bustin' out."

"Shoot," Alfred said, and tried to spit on the ground. His saliva landed, instead, on the front of his overalls. "This tinhorn joint can't hold the likes of me."

"That kind of attitude won't get you anything but a rope around your gullet," Slocum said.

Alfred stuck his tongue out at Slocum, his expression sour. "Don't you wish."

"Give me a day or two," Slocum said. "Maybe I will."

Slocum went across the street to the hotel and entered the dining room. There was an adjoining saloon through swinging doors and things sounded pretty lively for so early in the afternoon.

It wasn't hard spotting Perkey. The dining room was empty except for a pot-bellied, graying man of maybe fifty devouring a steak with all the trimmings. He had a bushy white moustache and sideburns, and the look of a man who'd seen his fair share of trouble, and more.

Slocum took off his hat and walked over to Perkey's table. Perkey didn't even look up from his meal, which he was devouring with gusto.

"Am I safe in assuming you're Marshal Perkey?" Slocum asked.

"His ownself," Perkey said, cutting his steak. "Help you?" He did not invite Slocum to sit down.

"Name's Slocum, John Slocum. I'm looking to scare up some bounty work if I can."

"Slocum, did you say?" Perkey asked, looking at Slocum for the first time.

"Heard of me?" Slocum asked.

Perkey shook his head. "No," he said, and went back to his meal. "Looking for some honest work, you say?"

"If there's any to be had," Slocum said.

Perkey pointed with his fork to the saloon. "Over yonder in the saloon you'll find a man who's wanted by the law. His buddies, too, most likely, though I ain't never seen their faces before."

Slocum went to have himself a look. He peered through the swinging doors and saw three men standing at the bar drinking heavily and laughing loudly. Slocum saw they were all three hardcases, sporting bad attitudes, and .45 Peacemakers with cutaway trigger guards. Slocum recognized the one in the middle, a short, wiry little weasel named Jiggs McKinney. He'd seen McKinney's ugly mug on wanted posters from Kansas to New Mexico Territory. He was wanted for bank robbery, cattle rustling, a few murders, and sodomy, though the posters thankfully failed to elaborate on that charge. Real white trash.

Slocum went back to Perkey's table. Perkey had finished wrestling with the steak and was now on his pie and coffee.

"Jiggs McKinney," Slocum said. "A very bad boy."

"I've killed worse, but not many," Perkey said.

"Why don't you arrest him, then?" Slocum wanted to know.

"Ain't finished my dessert yet," Perkey answered taking a sip of coffee. " 'Sides, he ain't broken no laws here in Roseville."

"Ain't broken 'em *yet*," Slocum corrected. "What's the reward on his miserable hide?"

"Two-hundred and fifty, last time I checked," Perkey said. "Thinkin' of takin' on three guns?"

The sound of exploding gunshots echoed through the saloon into the dining room, followed by whooping, hollering, and more gunfire. McKinney and his buddies were ventilating the ceiling. Slocum started toward the swinging doors, but Perkey was up in a flash, dropping his napkin down onto the table and holding out an arm to keep Slocum back.

"Sit, stranger, I'll handle this," Perkey said and started moving. McKinney and his friends were pouring rotgut down their gullets and taking turns blasting the piano. The piano player, a short little man, was huddled behind a nearby table. All of the bar's patrons had either dived for cover or made hasty exits.

"Another bottle!" McKinney bellowed drunkenly. A hand clutching a full bottle of whiskey appeared from behind the bar and plunked it down, then disappeared.

Perkey stepped through the double doors, and stopped. The tips of his fingers brushed over his Colt's pearl handle. The bearded weasel to McKinney's left was just about to take a hefty belt of whiskey when Perkey said, "I think you've had enough, boys."

McKinney turned slowly and sized up what passed for the law in Roseville. He grinned, showing teeth that looked like rotten cheese, and grabbed the upturned bottle from his friend. He tipped the bottle and gulped down half of the rotgut.

McKinney belched and wiped his mouth. He flung

the empty bottle at Perkey, but it hit the floor and shattered at his feet instead. Perkey didn't even flinch, and kept his gaze locked on McKinney. Perkey had guts, Slocum thought, now standing on the other side of the swinging doors and watching just for the hell of it.

"Another bottle," McKinney growled, and the hand, shaking badly now, appeared from behind the bar and set another brown bottle down. McKinney yanked the cork out with his teeth and spat it onto the floor. He took a big swig and shattered the bottle against the bar.

"Maybe I ain't had enough," McKinney said, wielding the jagged glass. "You gonna stop me, old man?" His left hand dropped slightly.

Perkey reached for his weapon. So did both of McKinney's pals. Before Perkey could even clear his holster, three shots rang out behind him. Perkey watched amazed as a red hole appeared in the middle of McKinney's forehead. He realized he hadn't even fired as the men on either side of McKinney crumpled to the floor at the same time, hit respectively in the gut and the heart. McKinney had the poor taste to stagger a few steps in a grotesque dance of death with blood and brains spurting from the hole in his head, and crash dead onto a table, sending bottles and glasses flying.

Perkey turned slowly, just in time to see Slocum holstering his Colt even before the gun smoke disappeared.

Slocum said, "Sorry if I got blood on the floor."

"Better theirs than mine," Perkey said. "Pretty fair shootin', stranger. Can't say I've ever seen such."

Slocum shrugged modestly.

"Had your dinner yet?" Perkey asked.

"Matter of fact I ain't," Slocum said.

"Have a seat." Perkey escorted Slocum to his table, then called over his shoulder to the bartender, "Tend to those bodies, Feeney. Get Stoon the undertaker."

"Okay, Chester," replied a voice from behind the bar.

Slocum and Perkey sat at the table. Slowly, the dining room staff began to reappear. Perkey called to an elderly, slightly idiotic-looking woman wearing an apron. "Amelia," he called to the waitress. "The best steak in the house for Mister Slocum, and bring us a bottle."

"Yes, Marshal," Amelia said, and shuffled off to the saloon, muttering, "Men and their guns. Blood everywhere, and guess who gets to clean it up. . . ."

After she returned with a bottle of whiskey and two glasses, Perkey poured them each out a drink. They clinked glasses and Perkey said, "Thanks for saving my bacon, Slocum. Not that I couldn't have handled it alone—"

"I just didn't like the odds," Slocum said as they tossed back their drinks. "When can I get the reward money?"

"What's your rush?" Perkey said, pouring them out another. "I could use some help around here. I ain't as young as I used to be, and my trigger finger ain't as limber, neither." Perkey took a swallow of his whiskey and added, "Besides, now that the railroad's going to be comin' through in a few months, Roseville'll be needin' all the law it can get. This town's going to grow by leaps and bounds, and when one honest man shows up with money, there's a half dozen more who try to take it from him. Why, when I was your age—"

"Cut to the chase," Slocum interrupted.

"I'm offerin' you a job, Slocum."

"In other words," Slocum said, "you're looking for a deputy marshal."

"Not in other words, yours'll do just fine," Perkey said. "I could use a man what won't dry up and blow away at the first sign of trouble." Perkey poured them out another. "Good help is hard to find these days. Mostly I get a bunch of snot-nosed kids who've read too many dime novels and can't separate the myths from the bullshit. That's not what I need, Slocum. The day of the gunfighter has passed, or so they tell us. These days, words speak louder than lead. What I need is a man with a silver tongue and maybe a few silver bullets . . . just in case. A man who can talk his way out of a gunfight but still shoot if his back is up against the wall."

"Not interested," Slocum said as Amelia brought out his dinner. He picked up his knife and fork and went to work. "I'll take my reward money and be on my way."

"It'll take a week for the reward money to get here from Dallas," Perkey said. "Maybe longer if I forget to wire them the request."

Slocum ate, seemingly unconcerned. "Might at that," he said.

"Let me suggest something then," Perkey said. "Try the job on for size. You get bored, you're free to leave as soon as your money arrives."

"If what you say about the railroad coming through here is true," Slocum said, spearing a piece of steak, "I could take that reward money and invest it in some kind of business, a dry goods store, or maybe a livery stable. Make myself a small fortune. Why would I want to be your deputy for a few dollars a month?" He put down his knife and fork and said to Perkey, "Pass the salt, please."

Perkey passed the salt. "You'd have the personal satisfaction of knowing you'd be protectin' the good people of Roseville from the evils of mankind."

Slocum continued eating, looking thoughtful, as though he was considering Perkey's offer.

"Well?" Perkey asked.

"Pass the pepper, please," Slocum said.

Perkey grabbed the pepper shaker from across the table, then abruptly slammed it down.

"I ain't passin' nothin' 'til you give me an answer," Perkey said indignantly.

Slocum took the pepper shaker from Perkey. "Nothing personal, Perkey," he said. "This seems like an all right town, but I can't see any good reason to put down roots here."

At that moment, a very pretty, stylishly dressed brunette of about thirty burst into the dining room. She looked extremely upset, but somehow, her anger made her look even prettier. "Chester!" she yelled, zeroing in on the town marshal. "I heard there was a shoot-out! What the bloody hell is going on? If you—"

Perkey nodded in Slocum's direction. Slocum, in mid chew, looked up from his plate at the pretty woman. His eyes locked with her's, and the steak caught in his throat.

"Slocum," the woman gasped.

Slocum managed to swallow and croaked, "Hello, Rose."

Rose walked slowly over to the table. Her gaze never left Slocum, and his gaze never left her.

Slocum felt every last drop of blood in his veins drain down to his toes. His knife and fork, clenched in his fists, were suspended over his plate.

She grabbed the half-full bottle of whiskey, and smashed it hard down on Slocum's head. Slocum winced as the thick glass shattered against his skull, drenching him in rotgut.

"You bastard," she hissed.

"I see you two have already met," Perkey said.

3

"Good to see you again, Rose," Slocum said, picking shards of broken glass out of his hair. "You ruined a perfectly good steak." His choice cut was now swimming in a pool of whiskey and glass.

"Mister John Slocum and I have some old business to discuss," Rose said to the marshal, her face flushed red with anger. "If you don't mind, Chester—"

"Say no more," Perkey said, and got up to make himself scarce. "Two's company, three's a riot." He grabbed his hat and added, "Think about my offer, Slocum." To Rose he said, "I'd be obliged if you don't kill him, Miss Rose."

Rose pulled out a chair and sat. Though he hadn't seen her in nearly two years, she was just as beautiful as he remembered. The fire in her blue eyes still blazed brightly, and he could see her figure was still as shapely, judging from the way she filled out the stylish gingham dress. He'd bet dollars to donuts she still had the same knockout body underneath that could stop a cattle stampede cold, the same one he'd reluctantly left behind in Brushwood Gulch, Colorado on a wintry January evening.

"You look fine, Rose," Slocum said, trying to break the ice, which at this moment was probably six feet thick. He had, after all, run out on her. "Damn fine."

"Don't try to soft-soap me, John," she said. "I could cover you with tar and feathers and run you out of town if I wanted to."

"So what's stopping you?"

Her expression was one of anger, but her eyes told a different story. She still had it for him, Slocum knew. Despite this, he also knew to tread lightly. The woman had a temper like a hungry mountain lion.

"I still might, I haven't decided," she said. "Just answer me one question: Why? Why did you light out on me the night before our wedding?"

Slocum hesitated. True, he *had* sort of skulked out in the middle of the night the day before they had decided to become man and wife. Saddled his horse and took off faster than a fart in a blizzard, straight to Cheyenne. Didn't leave so much as a note, or even say goodbye. Rose had every reason to be furious, and judging from past experience, Slocum knew she'd put his tit in a ringer just to watch him squirm.

"It wasn't because I didn't love you," Slocum said. "Let's get that out of the way right now."

"That doesn't cut it, Slocum," she said, standing abruptly. She started to pace angrily, clutching a lace hankie. "You know, you damn saddle tramp," she went on, "if you'd come to me and said, 'Rose, I'm sorry, but I've still got some rambling left in me,' or even 'I can't bear the thought of settling down,' I'd have had a tough time with it, but I would have understood. Instead, you crawl out of bed in the middle of the night to go pee and when I woke up you were halfway to Mexico."

"Cheyenne," Slocum said. "I went north."

"There are some things I can never forgive," she said, "and one of them is leaving me in a lurch."

Slocum had never heard that expression before, but then, Rose Liebowitz was chock-full of expressions nobody had ever heard, like Cop a walk, Go hop a trolley, and I'm not as dumb as you look. Not to mention the barrage of Yiddish curses and insults that only Rose Liebowitz from New York City's Lower East Side spewed when her dander was raised. Slocum's favorite, roughly translated, was, "You should own a hotel with a thousand rooms and have a stomachache in each one."

She'd come west as a young girl with her father to escape the poverty and disease of New York's slums. They'd gotten as far as Little Rock, Arkansas, where her father found work as a tailor. He died not long after, and Rose, a very buxom fifteen-year-old, discovered that her feminine charms—she had the ability to drive most men wild with the swing of her hips—could be used to the utmost advantage. To that end, she went into the employ of one Jewel Moon, the most successful madam west of the Mississippi.

Whereas a life of love-for-hire destroyed most women by aging them prematurely and leaving them sucking whiskey bottles, Rose flourished in her new environment. She learned the overall business, and was always on the alert, attracting

the wealthiest customers. One of her regulars, a
wealthy wine merchant with a bad heart, expired
one night in her arms. Midnight Rose (her profes-
sional name; the word around Little Rock was that
she did her best work after twelve A.M.) was blamed,
and almost allowed herself to be run out of town—
until she learned that the dead merchant had left her
twenty thousand dollars in his will. His widow, a
prim and proper, dried out old battle-ax, threatened
to contest it.

Go ahead and try, Rose threatened back. She borrowed money from Jewel and hired the best lawyer
in Little Rock. Hearing this, and knowing her name
would be dragged through the mud if the case went
to trial, the widow backed down.

Rose had had enough of Little Rock. For all intents
and purposes, it was still a one-horse town. Rose had
grown tired of the gossipy old women who turned
their backs whenever she passed. She took her twenty thousand dollars and made her way to Colorado,
first to Denver, and then to the small town of Brushwood Gulch. There were plenty of saloons but not a
single cathouse, not even the dirty two-dollar cribs
one found in the mining towns to the north.

A few cash bribes to the Brushwood Gulch town
council got Rose the okay to open her establishment, Midnight Rose's Good Time Emporium. Rose
recruited only the prettiest, shapeliest girls, and,
sparing no expense, sank most of her fortune into
decorating the place, sending away to St. Louis for
only the finest furnishings. She hired a Chinese
chef from Denver named Wing Tip Shoo who could
prepare anything from Irish stew to chicken chow
mein. *If a man's willing to spend a hundred dollars*

for a good time, Rose reasoned, *then he ought to remember it.*

Next came the roulette wheels, faro games, and blackjack dealers. Rose made sure the games were as clean as the satin sheets on the beds.

Not surprisingly, Rose's establishment became a raging success. High rollers and generous business-men from as far away as Chicago and Kansas City became regular customers, paying handsomely for the pleasure of curling up with a nubile maiden for a night or two during their travels.

It was in April of the following year, Slocum remembered, that he'd come to Brushwood Gulch. He'd been tracking a pair of murdering outlaws, Elvin and Harley Kreeg, and was about to make his move on them in a saloon when the sheriff decided to butt in, and got himself killed. Slocum managed to finish off the Kreeg brothers, but unfortunately, the price on their heads dropped to nothing if Slocum brought them back to Kansas dead, which Harley and Elvin definitely were. The good people of Wichita wanted to see firsthand the Kreeg brothers dance on air, as they'd cut a wide swath of murder and mayhem through the town. They weren't paying for corpses to hang.

Midnight Rose was impressed with the way Slocum handled himself in a gunfight and later, the way he handled her in bed. She offered Slocum a percentage of her business, and the town merchants offered percentages as well, to become the law in Brushwood Gulch. It was an offer he accepted, espe-cially when the bonuses included six nights a week in Rose's arms.

Slocum was in love, or so he thought. Midnight

Rose started talking about having babies and building a house outside of town. Somewhere along the line, he must have proposed—though Slocum was hard-pressed to remember exactly where and when— probably after one of their all-night sessions between the sheets. The thought of marriage made him want to run faster than a weasel in a chicken coop. Before he knew it, Slocum was headed to Cheyenne. Running from love had always been a way of life, and not even Rose's could hold him down.

Slocum figured he'd have a better chance of finding an honest poker game in Laredo than meeting up with Rose Liebowitz in the ass end of west Texas. But here she was, glaring at him, her face contorted in rage, but still as sweet as the night he'd run out on her nearly two years before.

"Why'd you do it, Slocum?" she asked softly, pain cracking her voice. "Why'd you run out on me?"

" 'Cause I'd have left you sooner or later," he said, "and that would have hurt more."

Rose sank wearily into a chair opposite him.

"You know something, Slocum?" she said. "You're a real horse's *tuchas*."

"You got every right to be riled at me," Slocum said. "I reckon I just ain't the marrying kind." He took off his hat and picked the shattered glass off it. "I was fixin' to tell you, I swear I was. I mean, things happened kind of fast. One minute we're having a good time together and the next you're drawing up plans for a house and how many kids we gonna have. Scare a man half to death."

"Not a real man," Rose said.

"Yeah, well . . . whatever," Slocum said. "I did what I did and I'm right sorry, Rose. I don't suppose you'll ever forgive me. No reason why you should. Under ordinary circumstances I'd move on out and let you get on with your life. Unfortunately, I've been detained by business."

He stood and jammed on his hat. "As soon as my reward money comes in—Perkey said about a week—you won't see my coattails for the dust. In the meantime, I'll make myself scarce to you."

He headed for the door, but halfway there Rose called out, "Where the hell you think you're going?"

"Thought I'd get myself a room at the hotel."

"With what?" she asked. "You don't have the price of a sandwich."

"There's four saloons in this town," he said. "Should be able to find a poker game in one of them. I'll get a stake."

"The way you play poker," she said, "I wouldn't bet on it." She shook her head sympathetically. "Go get yourself a room. Tell Freddy the clerk you're a friend of mine."

"I'm obliged to you," Slocum said. "I promise I'll stay out of your way."

"You don't get off that easy," Rose said. "Go upstairs and wait for me."

"And then what, Mommy? Do I get a spanking?"

"Just tell Freddy to send up a bottle of champagne and give me half an hour," she said. "It wouldn't look respectable if we went up together. I have my reputation to think of, you know."

"Must do an awful lot of thinking," Slocum murmured.

Before she could respond, he was out the door and crossing the dusty street to the Rose Hotel. The name Rose seemed to be prominent in the town of

Roseville. Somehow, Slocum didn't think it was a coincidence.

Inside the hotel, a tall, gaunt young lad of maybe twenty sat on a stool behind the front desk, snoring soundly—Freddy, no doubt. Slocum hit the bell. Freddy snorted twice and continued to doze. Slocum hit the bell harder, but Freddy didn't even stir. Slocum grabbed Freddy's left suspender, pulled it as far as he could, and released it. The suspender slapped Freddy firmly in the chest, flinging him backwards, and sending him crashing to the floor. He awakened and shook his head.

"What you do that fer?" Freddy asked indignantly.

"Fer nappin' on the job when you got an open cash drawer." He pointed to the hundred dollars in silver and bills. "Where I come from, that's known as stupidity. Don't know what it's called here. Do you, partner?"

Freddy slammed the drawer shut and said, "You looking for a a room or do you just like bothering folks?"

"I love to do both, but my time is limited," Slocum said. "Which room gets the best breeze?"

Freddy said, "Depends which night they serve the four-alarm chili at the cafe, and how many of our guests et it."

Slocum sighed. "They serving it today?"

Freddy said, "Yeah, they are. Course, room twelve is closest to Mister Drake's bakery. When his pies are bakin', it sorta compensates for the chili."

"Then give me room twelve," Slocum said, holding out his hand for the key.

"That'll be two dollars in advance," Freddy said,

eyeing Slocum suspiciously now. "*Sir.*"

"Miss Rose Liebowitz sent me," Slocum said. "She owns this establishment, I believe."

Freddy went pale and swallowed hard. "W-why didn't you say so?" He handed Slocum the key and added, "Anything you need, you give a holler."

"Just a bottle of champagne," Slocum said. "Put it on Midnight Rose's tab."

"Yes, sir," Freddy said. Slocum turned to leave. "Oh, and sir?" Freddy called.

Slocum turned to look back. Freddy motioned for Slocum to come closer and whispered, "She don't like to be called *Midnight* Rose."

"Since when?"

"Can't say when or even why," Freddy replied. "All I know, I seen Miss Rose slap down more than one poor bastard for addressin' her that-a-way."

"Sounds like I got somethin' to look forward to," Slocum said. "Have a good day, boy—and stay awake."

Slocum went across the street to the barbershop for a bath, shave, and haircut. The barber, an amiable, cherubic middle-aged man named Cyrus Lawson, couldn't do enough for Slocum after hearing he was a friend of Miss Rose's.

"A lovely woman," Lawson chirped as he trimmed Slocum's hair. "A pillar of the community and a credit to her tribe."

"Tribe?" Slocum asked. "What is she, Comanche?"

"No, an Is-rea-lite," Cyrus said. "Ain't never seen one in these parts till she came to town a couple of years back."

"Where'd she come from?" Slocum asked, already knowing the answer.

"Colorado," Lawson answered. "I hear tell that she ran a profitable dress shop there."

"That a fact?" Slocum smiled under the lather.

"Owns most of the town, she does," Lawson said, scraping Slocum's chin. "Even changed the name from Armadillo Corner to Roseville. Miss Rose calls the shots in this town, yes she does."

"Must've sold a lot of dresses," Slocum said.

Lawson was shaving Slocum's left cheek. He was an excellent barber; Slocum barely felt the razor. He was also a talking machine; he guessed Lawson would make idle chatter with a wooden Indian.

"Dresses indeed," Lawson snorted, then lowered his voice. "I heard that it was really a cathouse she was running."

"Do tell."

"Comes from back east," Lawson said. "New York." Lawson wiped the lather from the blade on his white apron. "Hot towel?"

"Why not?" Slocum said.

He wrapped the steaming towel around Slocum's face. The wet heat seeped into his flesh. It hurt and felt good at the same time, a lot like most of the women he'd known.

"Yes, sir," Lawson said. "Put this town on the map, she did. Wasn't but a few ramshackle buildings here, a saloon, and a mercantile, and a church. Miss Rose arrived, built the hotel and the cafe and somehow persuaded the railroad to come through here instead of Wolf Flat—all in less than a year. Town's been growin' by leaps and bounds ever since."

"Sounds like one smart lady," Slocum said.

"Smart can't even begin to describe her," Lawson said. He pulled the towel from Slocum's face. "All done."

"What do I owe you?" Slocum said, reaching into his pocket.

"For friends of Miss Rose," Lawson said graciously, "no charge."

And so it went. Slocum next dropped into the mercantile for some tobacco. The clerk grinned broadly and handed Slocum a pouch of his finest. "On the house," he said. "A friend of Miss Rose's is a friend of mine." Obviously, word had spread quickly through town that Slocum was someone special to their Miss Rose, and he was being treated like royalty. Before long, Slocum was approached by every businessman in town, offering everything free from peppermint sticks to new horseshoes.

Instead, Slocum declined with gracious thanks and returned to the hotel. He was pleased to see that Freddy had supplied the champagne—two bottles, in fact. There were also plates of chocolates and fruit set out on the bureau.

Slocum sat on the bed and rolled himself a cigarette. He was just lighting it up when Midnight Rose opened the door and stepped inside.

"Hello," he said, squinting through the smoke.

Midnight Rose said nothing. She'd changed for the occasion, and was wearing a fancy red dress with a matching hat and parasol. Slocum's heart lurched, racing faster than a bobcat chasing a muskrat. The fading sunlight filtered through the starched curtains, illuminating her. *Jesus*, he thought, *she is beautiful*. He must have been blind to run out on her.

"Hello yourself," she said.

"Done forgot how pretty you were," Slocum said. "Don't suppose you got all the mad out of your craw yet, huh?"

"Some," she said, staring at him. "I was thinking about having you sweat out the rest."

"I'm here," Slocum said. "Most men would've lit out, if they were sane."

"But then, you aren't most men, are you?" she said.

"Would you be offended if this man gave you a kiss?" he asked. There was no denying the prickly heat smoldering in the small room. Slocum wanted her. He'd never forgotten her soft curves, the feel of her breasts sliding over his bare chest, and the way she felt cradled in his arms in the wee hours of the morning. Had he ever really stopped loving her? The topic was definitely open to debate.

"Why don't you try and find out?" she said.

Slocum stood and walked slowly toward her. She was hard to read at this point; her face held no expression. He knew it was catch as catch can.

He stopped about six inches away from her. His arms felt like lead, and suddenly he didn't know what to do with his hands. He took another tentative step toward her. Rose neither stepped away nor did she move toward him.

He slowly, carefully slid his arms around her and pulled her close, remembering how good she felt against him. Still, she showed no resistance, so Slocum planted his lips firmly on hers. Surprisingly, she returned the kiss, and gradually curled her arms around him and embraced him. Her lips parted slightly, and Slocum took the opportunity to slide his moist tongue into her mouth.

The kiss was long and passionate. Then before things could go too far, Rose broke away.

Slocum released her and grinned. "When I kiss 'em, they stay kissed."

Rose grinned as well, then brought her knee up and planted it squarely and forcefully in Slocum's groin. The air rushed out of his lungs and he bent over with an audible groan.

"And when I knee 'em, they stay kneed," she said.

Slocum staggered backwards into the table that held the two bottles of champagne. He grabbed one in his fist and popped the cork in seconds flat, still bent over and in agony from his bruised testicles.

He held the bottle out to her. "Champagne?" he squeaked, his voice a good three octaves higher than normal.

"No thanks," she replied, looking quite satisfied with herself.

Slocum tilted the bottle to his lips and gurgled down half of it, gulping hard. It helped ease the pain—a little. Everything below his waist was on fire.

He sank onto the bed, still clutching his lower region.

"Does this make us even?" he asked through gritted teeth.

"We're getting there," she said.

"Don't know if I'll make it," Slocum said.

Rose came and sat down next to him on the bed. She stroked his face gently, wiping the hair out of his eyes.

"John Slocum," she said softly, shaking her head

disapprovingly. "What's a girl to do with you?"

"Anything she wants, within reason," he said. "Still got a unique way of expressing yourself, Rose."

"You had it coming," she said, still stroking his face affectionately. "Far be it from me to make a man feel guilty, John, but you did a terrible thing."

"What you just did wasn't exactly kosher," Slocum said.

"Did you ever really love me, John, or were you just looking to get it wet, like every other sweaty, smelly cowpoke in the territory?"

"For what it's worth, Rose," Slocum said. "I loved you as much as I'll ever love any woman. Not havin' ever really loved anyone before, I got no basis for comparison."

"For a man with a lot of hard edges," she said, "your talk is smooth. In other words, Slocum, I'm not impressed."

"Oh, you're not impressed, huh?" Slocum snapped, jumping up abruptly. A sizzling slice of pain tore across his groin. "Well, excuse me."

He half-walked, half-limped over to the table and took another long swig of the bubbly. "All right, Rose, I surrender. You win. That's what you really wanted to hear, right?" Slocum dropped into a chair, nursing his sweetmeats, which felt like two pumpkins lodged in his gut. "Either kill me or leave me in peace. I'm giving you the choice. I won't again."

Rose stood. "So be it," she said, clutching her parasol. She walked to the door and opened it. "Just do me one favor, Slocum. Look deep inside yourself and tell me what you see. Tell me what you feel."

She turned to leave. Slocum called out, "How about my balls in my hip pocket, for starters?"

"Not good enough," she said, closing the door behind her.

4

At a little past three in the morning, Slocum was snoring peacefully, happily dreaming of Rose with her long, sinewy legs wrapped around him.

Instinctively, he awakened the moment he heard the intruder touch the doorknob of his room out in the hallway. He was up and alert and reaching for his holster, which was hanging from the bedpost, as a key turned in the lock. When the door opened and a shadowy figure stepped into the room, he took aim at the unwanted visitor's chest and barked out, "That's far enough!"

"Take it easy, Slocum," Rose's voice answered in the darkness. "I'm not on any wanted posters."

He heard her strike a match and light the candles on the table. She'd let her hair down and it swept across her shoulders. She was wearing a heavy blue coat that all but made her look twice her size. She shook out the match and dropped it on the floor.

"Can I help you?" Slocum asked, unconsciously pulling the stiffly starched bed sheet up over his naked body.

Rose unbuttoned her coat and gracefully let it fall to the floor. She was wearing only a thin, shiny satin nightgown underneath. Her plump red nipples jutted through the flimsy material.

"Would you like some company?" she asked softly.

"Depends," Slocum answered. "Will it hurt?"

"That's up to you," she said.

She came to the bed and slid on top of him. She pressed her lips hard against his as he curled his arms around her, drawing her down firmly. They kissed passionately as Slocum slid his hands up and down her slim, curvy body and over her firm buttocks.

"I missed you something terrible, Rose," Slocum gasped between wet, hot kisses.

"Stop lying and love me," she whispered back, and he did.

A few precious moments later she broke the kiss and rolled off of him. She opened the night table drawer, which contained a Holy Bible and some rope.

"What do we have here?" Slocum asked, somewhat suspiciously.

"Rope," she said.

"Who put it there?"

"I did, this afternoon when you were roaming around town," she said. She picked up the Bible. "I knew this was one drawer you'd never stick your nose into." She tossed one length of the rope onto his chest.

"What do I do with this?"

"Tie your right wrist to the bedpost," she said casually, as though it was the most natural thing in the world.

"Would I be out of line if I asked why?" Slocum said, picking up the rope. "I mean, you weren't planning on hog-tying and branding me, was you?"

"Nothing that crude, Slocum," she said. "You can trust me."

"If I trusted you, I wouldn't be asking," he said, binding his wrist tightly to the bedpost nonetheless. This woman, as much as he liked her, was tougher to navigate than the headwaters of the Powder River.

She grabbed his free wrist and tied it to the opposite bedpost faster than he could roll a cigarette.

Rose sat back and studied her handiwork. Slocum was securely fastened to the bedposts, looking somewhat confused. Still, it hadn't effected his excitement—his manhood stood at rigid attention.

"Good," she said. "Your *tuchas* belongs to me. Now bend your knees."

Slocum did just that. Rose folded her legs behind her and sat on his groin. She wore nothing underneath the nightgown. She shifted about on him, settling down on his member. Slocum could feel his temperature rise as she slid onto it.

"Whatever you're going to do, Rose, do it," Slocum said hotly. She was damn near making him crazy with lust. He tried, from force of habit, to grab her hips and slam her down onto his swollen pecker, then remembered he was tied to the bedposts. It was something he wasn't entirely comfortable with. He preferred to be on top of any situation—especially with members of the opposite sex. Her wicked grin and the gleam in her eye made him a bit nervous—but also twice as excited.

Rose lifted her bottom off of him, then lowered it

slowly so that the tip of his shaft penetrated her an inch or so. Slocum's breath caught in his throat.

"I want to talk to you," Rose said huskily.

"I ain't exactly in a talkin' mood," Slocum panted. He pulled at the ropes, and succeeding only in cutting off the circulation in his wrists. Rose raised up on her haunches, letting Slocum's shaft slip out, and then dropped down and engulfed him again. She repeated the process three times, causing beads of sweat to pop out on Slocum's brow. *Torture, that's what it is,* Slocum thought dimly, loving every second of it. He wanted nothing more than to thrust himself deeply into her. Rose had other ideas.

"We need more law in this town," she said, poised and ready above him. "Do me a favor and stick around a while."

"Why should I?" Slocum said, tugging at the ropes. His mind wanted his hands on her thighs, but his wrists couldn't comply.

"I'll make it worth your while," she said, and lowered herself down onto his erect penis—but only a third of the way, swallowing the tip and a little extra.

"I'll think about it," Slocum said, gnashing his teeth.

"Think harder," she breathed, and sank down on him another inch.

He grunted, sounding both in pleasure and in pain. "Let's finish this and we'll see."

"Finish it yourself," she said, and jerked upwards. Slocum slid out of her and groaned in protest.

He strained at the ropes, hating her, hating being her prisoner.

"If I ever get out of this alive," he gasped, breathing hard, "you're going to be extremely sorry."

She lowered herself down again. His member gently slid into her. "Take your openings where you can," she said, and teased him again. "Don't be a *schmuck*, John. Stay with me for a spell. I'll make it well worth your time. Besides," she added, slipping halfway down onto him again and giving him an internal squeeze, "where else are you going to find a woman like me?"

Slocum wanted to be deep inside her, and wanted it more than he'd ever wanted anything in his life. His passion continued to mount; everything below his waist wanted to explode. The more he struggled, the more the ropes cut into his flesh. This situation was, he thought with a touch of irony, getting out of hand.

And I waltzed right into it, he grimly reminded himself.

"You're not running out on me this time," she said. She continued to tease him, gracefully sliding her warm, wet womanhood over his shaft. Slocum shook his head to keep the sweat from running into his eyes. This was worse than being invited to Thanksgiving dinner and being served hardtack.

"For God's sake, Rose," Slocum said breathlessly, "either fuck me or forget me."

She was trying to rope him like a steer. Slocum tried to think of arid deserts, dry creek beds, coughing up blood; his hatchet-faced schoolteacher, Miss Crabtree; anything to keep from being aroused. His efforts were in vain. She slid down onto him, engulfing him completely.

"What do you say, Slocum?" she said.

He tried to wiggle his bottom, but Rose held firm. "I'll think about your offer," he said.

She started riding him. The pleasure was so intense, Slocum wanted to leap out of his skin. Those breasts; Lord how lovely they were, bouncing up and down. He wanted to cup them in his hands and gently squeeze her nipples between his fingers. So near, yet so far. She rocked and bounced up and down on his throbbing shaft; Slocum knew he wouldn't be able to hold off for long. Then, just as things were building to a very nice conclusion, Rose abruptly stopped.

"Think harder," she said.

"Devil woman," Slocum hissed. He'd been three thrusts away from exploding. "I'll stay a week, see if I like it. Now, would you please untie me and let's finish this."

Rose made a mistake. She took pity on him.

"All right, Slocum," she said, slipping off of him. "But only if you promise to be nice." She loosened the ropes. He shook his hands free and rubbed his sore wrists. Then he grabbed her around the waist and tackled her to the opposite end of the bed, pinning her down.

"I'll be so nice, it'll hurt," he said, holding her wrists against the bed. He ripped her nightgown right down the middle, and in the next second was prying her legs apart with his knees. Rose offered even less resistance, welcoming him willingly as he plunged into her. She wrapped her legs around him and embraced him tightly, rhythmically pushing her hips to meet his thrusts.

Slocum jammed his lips down onto hers, grabbing her face firmly but gently. Their tongues did a slow dance with each other. The passion mounted, and Slocum couldn't remember exactly when he'd wanted a woman more.

It was just like old times. Within a minute or so, Rose was her old self—wet, willing, and wild. Slocum knew he would not be able to delay his climax for long. Rose, too, was swept up in the uncontrollable throes of ecstasy, and moments before Slocum exploded deep inside her, she cried out and dug her painted fingernails into his back.

Riding the range is nothing like this, he thought, a huge grin stretching across his face.

When it was over, he rolled onto his back and wiped the thin sheet of sweat off his forehead, breathing heavily.

"Still know how to show a man a good time, Rose," he said.

"Only the men I like," she added.

"Reckon y'all kill the ones you love," he said.

"If I did," Rose countered, "your worthless ass would've been in Boot Hill long ago."

"And I guess you'd be putting flowers on my grave every day," he said.

"No, I'd be dancing on it," she said, rolling onto her side. She drew little circles in the hair on Slocum's chest with her finger. "So tell me, John," she said. "How's life been treating you since you ran out on me in Colorado?"

"I've had my ups and downs," he answered, "but I can tell yours has been pretty good."

"I can't complain," she said.

"Just how much of this town do you own?" he wanted to know.

"The question," she replied, "is how much I *don't* own."

"Okay."

"I sold the place in Brushwood Gulch for a bundle," she said. "Too many memories." She gave a clump of his chest hair a mildly painful tug. "I thought about going back to New York, but I've taken a liking to breathing clean air, and there was plenty of it in west Texas. This town was little more than a way station when the stage stopped and I laid eyes on it. Between the Irish and German newcomers, they couldn't decide to name it New Dublin or New Berlin. I decided maybe this quaint little hamlet had the potential to be more. My instincts were right on the money. This is harsh country, Slocum, but we're taming it, making it work. This is a good land, as fine and pure as its people. It's not such a bad thing, investing a future in Texas. You should try it some time, Johnny."

"If I had anything to invest, maybe I would," he said, not liking where this chat was leading.

"How would you like a ranch of your own, say two thousand head? And a piece of the four saloons? How's five percent sound?" She grabbed his chin and forced him to look her square in the eye. "I offered you the moon once, Slocum, and you spit in my eye. It's usually never I give any man a second chance."

"I'm honored," he said.

"Don't be," she said tightly. "It's just the way things happen between men and women."

"Do you come with the deal?"

"Don't get cute, John," she said. "You should pardon the expression, but we need somebody minding the store who's got *chutzpah*. A man such as yourself."

Slocum started to chuckle, and shook his head. "You know, Rose," he said, "I knew you'd get around to this, as always. Mixing business with pleasure. I guess some habits are harder to break than others."

She slapped him hard across the face, and her free hand was reaching for his sweetmeats again for purposes anything but pleasurable. He grabbed her hand and pushed her down onto her back, then got on top of her and held her down.

"When are you going to get it, Rose?" Slocum said. "When are you going to stop thinking like a whore and start thinking like a regular person? Why do you think I lit out on you two years ago? Not because I didn't love you, no, not by a country mile. I left because everything between us was an understanding, a business agreement, even our marriage. How do you think I felt when you hauled out that legal document awarding me nothing if we ever got divorced? I wasn't after your money, Rose. You question my trust, you question me. Hardly a foundation to build a good marriage on, don't you think?"

"Like I said, Slocum," she said, her voice cracking. "I'm giving you a second chance. You won't get a third."

"I'll tell you what," Slocum said, rolling her onto her stomach and grabbing her left wrist. "Let me tie *you* up and see how you fare up under pressure."

Before she could reply, he was binding her right wrist to the bedpost and sitting on her firm fanny. She offered no resistance, and even subtly encouraged him.

"A crippled calf could get free of this," she said, yanking her right wrist against the ropes as he tied her left one to the opposite bedpost.

Slocum tightened both ropes until she was securely bound. She was now, without a doubt, his bedpost prisoner.

"All right, John," she said, tugging at the ropes and spreading her legs, just in case. "You've had your fun. Now what?"

"Now nothing," he said, jumping up off the bed and grabbing his pants. He climbed into them and snatched his shirt off a chair. He slipped it on and started buttoning it, looking out the window. "Sun's coming up. Reckon I'll wander over to the cafe and grab some steak and eggs." He tucked his shirt in and zippered up his pants, then reached for his boots and sat down on the edge of the bed and pulled them on. "Could use some coffee, too."

"This isn't funny, John," she said, straining against the ropes now. The more she struggled to get free, the tighter the ropes got.

"Believe me, Rose," he said, strapping on his holster, "we'll both get a big laugh out of it later."

"My sense of humor stinks," she said, looking over her shoulder as Slocum finished dressing. "The joke's over, Slocum. Untie me."

"And deprive that jerk at the front desk the undeniable pleasure of seeing you butt-naked?" he said, putting on his hat. "Maybe I'll see you around." He slapped her shapely buttocks and went out the door.

"Slocum, if you walk out now you'll never see me—" he heard her yelp as he slammed the door behind him. He strolled casually down the hallway to the stairs, and was halfway down the first flight when he heard Rose bellow loud enough to wake every rooster in west Texas. Down in the hotel lobby, Freddy was faithfully fast asleep behind the desk. Slocum saw no reason to disturb him, though the urge to fire a shot into the ceiling was tempting. The dumb shit had left the cash drawer open again.

Slocum slammed it shut, not bothering Freddy's contented slumber, and stepped out onto the street. The sun was barely poking up behind the church steeple, but he could see the beginnings of life across the way at the cafe. He took one step off the wooden planks when he saw a cloud of brown dust streaking through the first few rays of sunlight down the street and heard the collective rumble of hooves. His back stiffened at the sound; there was at least three of them, and few stormed into any town at dawn who hadn't broken the law and were running from it.

A second or two later three men galloped into town, screaming in drunken glee and firing shots into the air. More prairie trash, Slocum decided. Most likely trouble for someone. No wonder Rose wanted more law in her town. The hell with her, Slocum decided. *I'm not staying.*

The three riders stopped in front of one of the saloons and hitched up at the post. As the dust settled, Slocum got a better look at the saddle tramp in the middle, did a double take, and looked again, just to be one hundred percent sure.

He was. His stomach dropped.

"Shit on fire and save the matches," he gasped. He turned and walked quickly back into the hotel. He bounded up the stairs, taking them three at a time, and returned to his room. He flung the door open. Rose was still there, trying to chew through the ropes.

"You stupid bastard," she hissed as he sat down on the bed and started untying her. "Just who the hell—"

"Shut up, Rose," Slocum said, cutting her off. "You got trouble, right here in Roseville."

"No, buster, you got trouble," she snapped as Slocum loosened the ropes. "If you think—"

Once free, she tried to slap him, but he was ready for her. He grabbed her hand and said, "Slug Fisher and two of his boys just rode into town."

The color drained from her face. "When?" she asked.

"Not two minutes ago," he said, sounding as serious as she'd ever heard him. "This could be a bad thing, Rose. Real bad."

"Damn *schlemiels*," Rose snapped.

"My feelings exactly," Slocum said.

5

Slocum escorted Rose down the street to Hiram Quick's house, at the far end of Main Street. Hiram owned half of Roseville's bank and also doubled as the town's mayor, or so Rose explained. Slocum knew that odds were good it was she who called most of the shots in the territory, especially when Hiram Quick came to the door. He was a tall, gaunt man with a huge Adam's apple the size of a peach, who leaned toward nervousness—hardly a leader of men. Slocum assumed he took his orders from Rose and rarely questioned them.

"Slug Fisher, you say?" Quick asked, half-shaven, his Adam's apple bobbing furiously, and his eyes bulging with fear. "Here in Roseville?"

"I'm afraid that's the case, Hiram," Rose said. "Get everyone over to the marshal's office as quickly as you can."

Quick's beady eyes scanned Slocum up and down. "Who's this?" he asked Rose, though his eyes never left Slocum.

"His name's John Slocum," Rose said, grabbing

Slocum's arm and pulling him toward the jail. "He's on our side."

Quick wasn't wholly convinced. He eyed Slocum suspiciously. "Can he do us any good or is he just around for show?"

Slocum felt his dander rise. He wasn't usually this thin-skinned but there was something about this Hiram Quick's attitude that rang a wrong chord in him. Slocum decided he didn't care for this skinny church mouse of a man. He took a menacing step forward to challenge him, but Rose held him back. "Just do as I say," she snapped at Quick. "Meet us in ten minutes."

She grabbed Slocum's arm, and together they turned to leave. He took her lead as they walked across the street toward the jail. Slug Fisher and his friends had disappeared into the Wilted Daisy Saloon to wet their whistles, and God only knew what else. Slocum knew as well as Rose did that it was only a matter of time before gunshots would start piercing the early morning breeze. Time was of the essence.

Perkey was sacked out in his chair behind his desk. To the left, a coffeepot gurgled from the faint heat of a potbellied stove. Inside the cell, an old geezer with a month's worth of whiskers snored on one of the bunks.

"Get up, Chester," Rose snapped. Perkey's eyes opened and he was on his feet in a flash, reaching for his firearm. Slocum managed a grin and relaxed just a bit. For a tired old man, Perkey seemed to be on the ball.

"Take it easy, Chester," Rose soothed.

"I'm plenty easy," Perkey said, looking at Slocum.

"Why did you interrupt my beauty sleep?"

"Slug Fisher just rode into town," Slocum said to the lawman. He grabbed the coffeepot off the stove and poured Perkey a cup. "You best drink some of this and get your wits about you." Slocum made no mention of the empty whiskey bottle in the wire wastebasket next to Perkey's desk.

Perkey dutifully drank the hot coffee. He said, "Slug Fisher, huh? Is Ma with him?"

"Not so I saw," Slocum said.

"Round up who you can," Rose said to the marshal. "Bring them back here."

"Yes, ma'am," Perkey said.

"Get word to all the ranchers in the territory," Rose continued, "make sure they know I want every one of them here as soon as possible."

"I'll do that, Miss Rose," Perkey said. He was out the door and mounting up in an instant.

Slocum and Rose turned to leave. The sleeping figure in the jail cell, not having moved an inch, said, "Was I you, I'd be roundin' up every gun in the county."

"Who the hell asked you?" Slocum said, feeling annoyed. He was being dragged into a situation he wanted nothing to do with. The longer he stayed around, the better his chances of being on the losing side of this battle.

"Nobody asked me, pecker head," the old geezer said, sitting up on the bunk and scratching his crotch through his long underwear. "I'm just suggestin'." He scratched his crotch again. "Seein' how's I once rode with Ma Fisher and her boys and know their evil ways. Though I don't suppose that would be interesting to y'all."

The old goat settled down onto the bunk and went back to sleeping off his latest hangover. His snores filled the small jail as soon as his head hit the pillow.

"Ever see this man before?" Slocum asked Rose.

"Of course I have," Rose snapped. "That's our town character, Geezer McDougall."

"I think he's somebody we should talk to," Slocum said. "Wake up, old man!" Slocum yelled.

Geezer didn't budge. He snored like a buzz saw. Slocum was about to yell again, but Rose said, "Forget it, John. If I know Geezer—"

Before she could finish, Slocum was already grabbing the fire bucket full of water in the corner. He said, "Where does Perkey keep the keys to the cells?"

"Come on, Slocum," Rose said a bit too dryly. "Where do you think they are?"

Slocum sighed tiredly and opened the bottom drawer of Perkey's desk. Underneath a sheaf of yellowed papers were the keys. Some things never changed. Slocum was impressed, though, that Rose knew about the keys. He liked a woman who stayed on top of a situation—some situations, anyway.

Grabbing the bucket, he went to the cell where Geezer McDougall was sleeping soundly. He unlocked it and was about to fling the water onto Geezer when the toothless varmint rolled over, totally awake, and said, "Watch it with that water, son. This ain't Saturday night."

"It is for you unless you feel like talking," Slocum said, still poised with the bucket. Geezer blinked twice. Slocum thought the old prairie tramp looked like one big liver spot. Slocum asked, "You said you rode with the Fishers?"

"I oughta know what I said," Geezer snapped impatiently.

"Prove it," Slocum said.

"Been more'n ten years since I fired a shot for the Fisher bunch," Geezer said, "but I don't imagine much has changed since then. As long as Ma Fisher is breathing, the murder rate in this territory'll climb higher than the Tetons." Geezer yawned and added, "Never knew what true evil was 'til I rode with 'em. Ma Fisher, well, that old gal is lower than a snake's toes. Bore herself thirteen sons and done buried half of 'em, and they all died from lead poisoning. Was with 'em for six months, and that was six months too many. The Fisher bunch got a lust for bloodlettin' that would leave Genghis Khan green with envy."

Geezer settled back onto the cot and made himself comfortable. "No, sir," he said, looking Slocum square in the eye. "Ma Fisher and her brood decide to pay you a visit, you best pack up and head for anywhere they ain't."

"Are they that bad?" Rose asked hoarsely.

"That bad and worse," Geezer said.

Rose went and sat down on a wooden bench. She'd dressed quickly, and forgotten her handkerchief. It was barely seven in the morning, but already the west Texas heat had her perspiring. It was hotter than the worst August day on the Lower East Side of New York, she thought, where the brick tenements sucked up the sun and raised the temperature by fifteen degrees.

She had heard of the Fisher gang, but only

thirdhand, in parlors and dining rooms, and through the drunken boasts of horny cowboys and gunslicks who'd spoken of their violent exploits throughout Oklahoma Territory. The very thought of the Fishers wreaking their deadly brand of havoc on Roseville did not make her happy.

"What do we do?" she asked Slocum.

"*We?*" Slocum said. "Who's *we?* I don't remember being part of this particular equation."

Rose looked at him sharply and said, "I don't have time for this, John. If you want to help me, then help me. If not, be on your way and there will be no love lost between us—that is, what hasn't been lost already."

"You want me to stay?" Slocum asked.

Rose said, with bravado Slocum knew she didn't have, "Do whatever the hell you want. I've been through tougher than this."

"You ain't been through tougher than the Fisher gang," Geezer said. Slocum realized he was still ready to douse him with the bucket's contents. He put it down and sat on the end of the bunk.

"Tell me more about these Fishers," Slocum said.

"What I can offer ain't nothing you ain't heard before, most likely," he said, sitting full up on the bunk. He got up and grabbed the bars of the jail cell. "I won't swear on it, but I think this town's just got itself a snootful of trouble. You got any objection to me gettin' out of here and takin' a much-needed leak?"

"Not before you tell me what I need to know," Slocum said. The cell door was wide open; Geezer could leave any time he wanted to.

"Could be Slug and his buddies just rode in for a

good time and'll go about their business," Geezer commented.

"Could be," Slocum said, and turned to Rose. "This town got a whorehouse in it?"

"What the hell do you think?" she said sharply.

"Then maybe that's all they came for," Slocum said. "That, and to raise some hell in Roseville's saloons. Maybe they'll leave," he added hopefully, but his heart wasn't in it. His gut told him that hope was a luxury none of them could afford. He'd never gone up against Ma Fisher and her brood—few did and lived to tell about it. Their reputation struck terror into the hearts of men, women, and children from the Bitterroots to the Brazos River. They'd killed more than a dozen lawmen, even some federal marshals Slocum had known. And despite the fact that the Fishers had been subject to numerous ambushes and had even shot it out with a regiment near Fort Kearny, Nebraska, Ma Fisher always seemed to get away clean with only a son or two dead to show for it. Recruiting fresh blood never seemed to be a problem. There was plenty of prairie scum and half-breed trash around to replace the fallen Fisher gang members.

"What are the odds Ma and the rest of her murdering devils'll come through?" Slocum asked Geezer.

Geezer pulled a matchstick out of his pocket and chewed on it thoughtfully.

"Better'n even," he said. "Was me, I wouldn't lay a penny down they'd likely ignore a prosperous town such as this 'un."

"I can't believe it," Slocum said, and felt strangely tired. "Last I heard, they were raiding one-horse shitholes in Kansas and Missouri. How the hell they get this far south so soon? It wasn't but a month ago they were wanted in Stockton."

"Oh, they's been invited to a hefty share of hangin' parties," Geezer said, "but they declined to attend."

He shook his head wearily and sighed. Slocum saw a man who knew his days were definitely numbered. His insides were rotting from cheap liquor and a steady diet of beans and bacon, but his mouth and his memory still worked like new. "Yes, sir," he said, "if the devil's got hisself a mother, it's more likely'n Missus Charity Fisher."

"*Charity?*" Rose asked.

"Kinda amusin' when you think about it," Geezer said. "Only charity she believes in is her ownself."

"All right," Slocum said, his jaw set grimly. "How many Rangers are there in these parts?"

"Take five days before even one of 'em could get here," Geezer said. "If the Fishers come, it'll damn well be before then."

"Why don't we wire the federal marshal in San Angelo?" Rose asked. "Surely he'd be interested in catching the Fisher gang."

Slocum shook his head. "Same difference. Ain't but four federal marshals in this part of Texas, and they're each responsible for thousands of square miles. No, experience tells me we're on our own."

Geezer said, "Town this size against Ma Fisher? We're in over our heads. Between 'em, the Fishers got more lives than a passel of cats. I should know."

"Exactly," Slocum said. "That's why you're the one who's going to talk to Slug Fisher and find out where the rest of the gang is holed up."

"No thanks, friend," Geezer said. "Breathin's gotten to be a bad habit with me, but I'd like to continue all the same. I left the Fishers for a reason and a damned good one. I been surrounded by a dozen bloodthirsty Comanche, been swept down rain-swole rivers on my horse, faced off a half a dozen *pistoleros* in a Meskin cantina, and rode shotgun on a stage through Apache country. But ain't nothin' in this whole wide world scared me nearly as much as the Fisher bunch. I'll help y'all if I can—I'm still pretty handy with a Sharps—but ain't too many men can look Slug Fisher in the eye and not get a bullet in it."

"I'll be right behind you," Slocum said.

"Then that'll be two of us to bury."

Rose looked scared. Slocum couldn't fault her for it. "You could talk to him, Geezer. You're his friend," she said.

"Slug Fisher ain't got no friends," Geezer said. "Only victims."

"You're about as threatening as a baby armadillo," Rose insisted. "And about as dangerous as a mosquito bite. This Slug person won't have any reason to kill you. I bet he won't even harm a hair in your ear."

"If you're trying to build his confidence, Rose," Slocum said, "you're doing a lousy job."

Rose ignored him, then she stood and walked toward the cell. She was springing into her shrewd business side. Slocum allowed himself a grin. When Rose went to work on a body—and he knew from firsthand experience—she didn't let up until they were exhausted. The power of pink, or money, or both tended to wear a man down.

Rose wisely went for the money. She said, "Would a hundred dollars change your mind?"

Slocum's gaze turned to Geezer. The old goat was playing it close to the vest, looking noncommittal, and chewing his matchstick. Geezer McDougall, Slocum decided, had seen Rose in action before.

Geezer said, "Way I got it figured, Miss Rose, I got me maybe three years of livin' left in me before either my liver or my ticker calls it quits. What you're offerin' works out to about thirty-three dollars a year, and I like to think my life is worth a hell of a lot more than that."

Rose shrugged and sat back down on the bench. "And just how much do you suppose one year of your life is worth, Mister McDougall?" Her expression was grim, but Slocum knew that she was, if only momentarily, enjoying the negotiations. Bargaining was in her blood.

"Cain't say I ever put any price on it," Geezer said.

"Try," Rose said. "I'll help you decide. What's the most you made in your best year?"

"Countin' or not countin' the rate of inflation?"

Rose smiled slightly, and Slocum knew she was almost impressed that Geezer even knew a word with more than two syllables.

"Whatever," Rose said.

Geezer pretended to think about it. "Made three hunnet gold pieces fer fightin' agin Maxie-million in Vera Cruz, Mexico, some years back. Figure that translates into five hundred American dollars today."

"Five hundred and ninety-three dollars and thirty cents to be exact," Rose said. "At least according

to the latest reports in the Houston newspapers."
She added, "I'll give you six hundred dollars for one
six-minute chat with Slug Fisher."

Geezer had never seen that much money at one
time in his life, Slocum knew. Still, the whiskery
old buzzard tried not to show it. "Is that what you
Yankee snake oil slickers call a profit margin?" He
grunted.

Rose pulled a tin of makeup from her purse and
started to freshen herself up. "Let me ask you one
question, Geezer," she said, and didn't wait for his
response. "Hasn't this town been good to you?"

"As towns go . . ." Geezer started.

"Who let you drink on credit in the saloons when
your credit wasn't worth a Confederate dollar?"

"You did," Geezer said.

Rose went to work in earnest. "Who lets you leech
drinks from everyone in town? Who gave you that
job shoveling out the stables? Who lets you sleep
here in our jail? Who gives you one meal a day,
sometimes two?"

Geezer seemed to shrink even smaller than he
was. His was a losing battle and he knew it. "You
did," he said, waiting for the crushing blow. It came,
but Rose wrapped it in velvet. "I'll arrange it so you
eat and drink for free the rest of your life," she said.
"And I'll give you four hundred in pocket money
besides."

"Throw in a goose down mattress," Geezer said,
patting the rotted straw one, "and you got yourself
a deal."

"Sold," Rose said with a smile, "but if you get
killed, the deal is off."

"Sounds fair enough," Geezer responded, and

immediately felt like he'd just sold his soul, lock, stock, and barrel.

•   •   •

"What do I say to him?" Geezer asked, as Slocum and Miss Rose, each holding an arm, personally escorted him down Main Street toward the Wilted Daisy, where Slug and his friends were sequestered.

"Make small talk," Slocum said, trying to sound convincing. "You know, the weather, the price of rustled cattle, how's Ma's gout? When does she plan to sweep through town, stuff like that." Chances were good he was sending Geezer into certain death, and Slocum wasn't comfortable with that fact.

"Fishers don't cotton to small talk," Geezer said. "They'd just as soon kill me dead for runnin' out on 'em."

"Don't worry," Slocum said. "I'll be right behind you."

"That ain't a comforting thought, exactly," Geezer said as they approached the saloon.

6

Geezer stopped at the wooden boardwalk in front of the saloon and clasped his hands together in prayer.

"Lordie," he said, looking up at the sky. "Don't take this personal, but I'd be beholden to you if you saw fit to spare my miserable hide one last time."

With that, he stepped onto the boardwalk and went into the saloon. Slocum loitered outside, leaned against a wooden post and rolled himself a smoke. It would make the Fisher boys nervous if two men walked in together. Geezer, even to the most timid soul, posed little threat.

Slocum lit the smoke and made his way to the wall beside the saloon's swinging doors. He took a little peek inside, just for the hell of it.

Slug Fisher and his buddies were sitting at a table polishing off a bottle. There was no conversation between them, only furtive glances at the door and at the other early morning drinkers. While not exactly at ease, their guard would be down after a few more rounds of rotgut.

Slug Fisher was a ferret-faced young pug of maybe

twenty. His features were plain to the point of being almost nonexistent so that he looked like a mental half-wit, as though whoever had fathered him had not been of superior breeding stock. Somewhere before Slug was conceived, the juice had thinned considerably. He and his buddies wore battered black overcoats in spite of the west Texas heat and about twelve layers of dirt and prairie dust. None of them had even remotely seen anything resembling a razor or soap and water in months.

Slug was toting what looked like a Remington .44. A fair weapon, Slocum knew, but better utilized when a body wasn't in a hurry. There was probably something in his boot as well, but it was the Henry .44 propped up against the table that worried Slocum more. Slug's two companions, Del Center and Nasty Nick, likewise sported some old but still reliable firearms from Smith & Wesson.

Geezer, entering the saloon, transformed himself into a stumbling drunk, a part he had years of experience playing. He staggered across the floor to the bar and slapped his hands down. A prudent move, Slocum reasoned. Slug and his pals were less likely to ventilate a harmless old drunk.

"Gimme a whiskey, Solly," Geezer said as loudly and drunkenly as he could.

Solly Dowd absently reached for a bottle behind him and slammed it down on the bar. He reached for a shot glass at the same time, never taking his eyes off the mean-looking trio at the table. He obviously gave no thought to the fact that Geezer had no money to pay for his drink. He looked apprehensive, spilling whiskey as he poured it into Geezer's shot glass.

"Whoa there, Sol," Geezer said jovially, pushing the bottle up. "No sense in wasting it, son."

Geezer spun around and faced Fisher. He downed the shot, slammed the glass onto the bar and loudly slurred, "Well, if it ain't Slug Fisher, my old buddy."

Geezer stuck out his hand and staggered over to the table. The man had balls of brass. Slocum allowed himself a small smile.

"Put it there, Sluggie," Geezer said jovially.

Slug regarded the old fart like a horse patty stuck to the heel of his boot. He worked on a wad of tobacco in his mouth and then shot a stream of brown juice onto the tattered cuffs of Geezer's pants.

Geezer looked hurt. "That's no way to treat a friend, Slug. It's me, Geezer McDougall."

Slug's eyes narrowed, as though the act of remembering was beyond his comprehension. A second or two later something appeared to dawn on him. He looked at Geezer and blinked a couple of times. "Don't ah know you?" he drawled.

"It's me, Slug—Geezer McDougall," Geezer repeated. "Used to run with you and your brothers and your ma. Did yer cookin'. Hell, I fattened you up on my biscuits when you were no bigger'n a baby possum and brewed your coffee when you were nary thirteen and already havin' hangovers."

"Old Geezer," Slug said, slowly remembering now. "Shore, I recollect the face. Ain't you one of my brother's daddies?"

"Can't say as I is," Geezer said. "What brings you to these parts, Slug?"

Slug totally ignored the question. "Run out on us somewhere around Salinas, if I recollect," he said, his hand dropping to his belt and gripping the handle of his gun. He spit another sloppy stream of tobacco juice out of the corner of his mouth.

"It wasn't such, Slug," Geezer said, no doubt wishing he was anywhere else, like, say, Paris or the Alps. "Tied one on in the saloon and passed out cold in a pile of sawdust, I did. When I waked up, you wuz all gone."

"Horseshit," Slug persisted. "You run out on us, was ten years back. Ain't nobody runs out on the Fishers." He clenched the butt of his gun and pulled it from the holster, pointing it at Geezer.

"Honest, Slug," Geezer said, swallowing hard. "Tried to catch up with y'all, but—"

"Never did like your biscuits, neither," Slug said with a glint in his eye, and pulled back the trigger. Geezer shut his eyes and waited for the inevitable.

"Kill 'im good, Slug," Del Center said, grinning.

Slocum came through the swinging doors and strode to the bar, diverting Slug's attention just long enough to keep the old buzzard breathing for the time being. Slocum leaned back against the bar and looked at Slug, whose gun was pointed squarely at Geezer's gut. Except for Solly and a big-eared, tall, gangly man of maybe twenty-one at the end of the bar, plus a couple of derbied drummers at one of the other tables, the place was deserted. They all looked pretty scared and understandably so. Slug Fisher and his friends were some nasty-looking sons of bitches.

"Hope I ain't interruptin' nothing," Slocum said amiably. He turned to the bar. "Solly," he said to the jittery bartender, "whiskey."

The men on either side of Slug instinctively sat up erect, on the alert now. Slocum never took his eyes off them, sizing them up. Even if he managed to get two of them, there was always the third. Rotten odds.

"Just a family squabble, señor," Nasty Nick said. "Ain't that right, Slug?"

Slug didn't respond. He stared back at Slocum, who saw curiosity, hate, and maybe even a little bit of fear in Slug's eyes. Slocum was smiling slightly; a cold smile more than anything could put the fear of God into the hearts of most men.

"Sure hope you wasn't planning on killing that old billy goat," Slocum said. "Kinda hard finding able bodies to shovel horseshit at the stables." Solly set a whiskey down on the bar. Slocum reached back and grabbed it, his gaze never leaving Slug's. "Unless one of you boys would like to take his place. Lord knows, with your stench, you're halfway there."

Slug's companions squirmed in their chairs, wanting to jump up and draw on this arrogant stranger. Instead though, they waited for their leader to make the first move; bloodthirsty red worker ants, all venom.

Slug poured himself out a shot and said, "You callin' me some sorta shit kicker?"

"If the shit kicks, wallow in it," Slocum said, still grinning.

Geezer looked back and forth at Slug and Slocum; he watched as the barrel of Slug's pistol moved slowly away from him and over to Slocum. Slug had bigger fish to fry now; Geezer took the opportunity to fade into the woodwork.

An expression of pure rage swept over Slug's face. He lurched up from his chair, and trained the barrel of his gun on Slocum's chest. Slocum knew the play:

Slug's movement would be a signal to his buddies to start pumping lead, leaving Slocum to deal first with them and giving Slug the chance to blast Slocum's head into a bloody stub.

True to form, they jumped up at Slug's cue but never even cleared leather. Slocum drew and pumped two shots into Del Center's belly. He flew backwards into the next table. Slocum heard two shots ring out behind him, and Nasty Nick crumpled backwards and joined his friend, the bullets blowing off part of his head. Gray and red meat and chunks of skull exploded all over a fake French painting of a naked lady on the wall. The two drummers dove out of the way of the flying lead.

Slug looked momentarily confused, his attention diverted to the tall shooter at the bar. Slocum aimed at Slug's heart while he had the chance and was about to squeeze the trigger when, from behind Slug, Geezer appeared out of the shadows wielding a rickety wooden chair. He brought it neatly down onto Slug's head. It shattered into at least ten pieces as Slug crossed his eyes and sank down unconscious to the floor, his six-shooter skidding across the sawdust.

"Don't you dare shoot that boy, Slocum," Geezer said, holding the remains of the chair. "You do and we'll fer sure have the Fisher gang breathing down our necks."

Slug's buddies were already drawing flies. Slocum glared at Geezer and holstered his Colt. He turned and saw the tall, gangly man at the bar holster his gun as well.

"Reckon I owe you a drink," Slocum said to him.

"Weren't nothing," said the man—though he was

barely old enough to be one. He moved down the bar and brought his empty glass with him. "Man wants to buy me a drink, Solly."

Solly slowly rose up from behind the bar, and shakily poured shots into each of their glasses.

Slocum raised his glass in a toast. "Name's Slocum," he said. "John Slocum, and I'm obliged to you."

"Dennis Mallory," the fresh-faced man said. "Got me a ranch a few miles outside town." They clinked their glasses.

"Luck," Slocum said.

"Luck," Mallory said, and they knocked them back.

Solly poured them each another without being asked. Geezer dropped the remains of the chair and bellied up to the bar. "Gimme what they're having," he told Solly.

"You ain't got no money, you old buzzard," Solly said.

"Give the man a drink," Mallory said to Solly. "It's on me."

Solly produced a glass and poured Geezer a shot. Slocum paid for the second round as well. There weren't many men you could count on when the shit started flying; Dennis Mallory seemed to be one of them. Slocum liked that.

"To your health, boys," Geezer said, and downed his drink.

"Give the man another," Slocum said, and Solly did. "Pretty handy with that Peacemaker, Mister Mallory," he said to his new friend.

"Used to shoot crows back in Tennessee," Mallory said.

"Make sure he's out for the time being," Slocum said to Geezer, motioning with his glass at Slug Fisher's inert form on the floor.

"Don't worry, he's out cold," Geezer said, and sipped his whiskey. "Them Fishers got hard skulls, but ain't one of 'em could stop an oak chair."

"Did he say Fisher?" Mallory asked, sounding a little less confident now.

" 'Fraid so," Slocum said.

"Just be glad the murderin' young devil's still breathin'," Geezer remarked. "Alive, the chances of the Fishers comin' here are fifty-fifty," he said. "Dead, Ma Fisher will burn this town to the ground and laugh while she's strikin' the first match. Ma don't cotton to her sons gettin' killed."

"Didn't have no idear the Fishers were prowlin' these parts," Mallory said nervously, tossing a silver dollar onto the bar. "When that one wakes up, it's my face he'll see. I best be on my way."

Slocum said, "Hold on there, Mallory. Ain't nothing to be afraid of just yet." Slocum turned to Geezer. "What do you suggest we do with him?" he asked, pointing to Slug Fisher.

Geezer downed his second drink and looked thoughtful as he stared at Slug's motionless body. "Hard one to call," Geezer said. "Slug's going to be madder than a swarm of hornets when he comes to. He don't show up soon, Ma will fer sure come here lookin' for him."

"Then we bring him to and send him on his way," Slocum said. "With a message to his people to stay the hell out of Roseville. That we got guns and we're willing to use them. Convince him that the town of Roseville is better left alone."

"That'll just piss him off even more," Geezer said. "Was I you, I'd apologize to Slug and try to make amends. Send him away in a good humor and hope he don't lead the rest of his brood down here. Best we can hope for. With any luck, Ma and her boys'll bypass Roseville altogether."

"I think Geezer is right," Rose said, coming through the bat-wing doors. She looked down at the dead bodies on the floor. "I think we need to appeal to Slug Fisher's sense of decency."

"Decency?" Slocum asked, and looked at her. "This isn't the Lower East Side of New York where you sit down with someone and negotiate over a glass of seltzer. You pander to this scum," he said, "and you're asking for a heap of trouble. Send him on his way and prepare for the worst."

"And I say we treat him nice and hope for the best," Geezer said.

"And what about the two we killed?" Mallory asked.

"They ain't blood kin," Geezer said. "Nobody's gonna lose any sleep over 'em. We just apologize to Slug and—"

"Apologize?" Slocum snorted. "Ought to string his worthless ass up."

"Geezer's right," Rose said hopefully. "If we let him go—"

"The only place he's going is to jail," Slocum said. "And when he comes to, I want to have a chat with him."

"We don't need you killing him, John," Rose said.

"Just let me have a little heart to heart with him, that's all," Slocum said grimly. Rose knew the look; it was Slocum's *I'm through arguing* look.

"Best be keeping your hands off his throat," Geezer suggested.

Slocum bent and grabbed Slug's pistol off the floor. He went outside and fired two shots into the air, then shoved the gun into his belt and went back into the saloon.

"Trust me," Slocum said. "I got an idea."

"God help us," Rose murmured.

"That's a chunk of what I'm hoping for," Slocum said.

7

Slocum, Geezer, and Mallory carried Slug Fisher over to the jail and plopped him down onto a bunk. Rose followed behind, barking out instructions. She was a sweet woman, Slocum knew, but she could also be a serious pain in the butt sometimes. All three grunted as Slug crashed unconscious onto the thin straw mattress. Carrying a body was a lot like carrying a sackful of lead. Slocum slammed the cell door and locked it.

"Mallory," Slocum said to the young rancher, "you got a family?"

"My wife and my baby girl," Mallory said.

"You best be getting back to them," Slocum said. "Now."

"Why's that?" Mallory asked cautiously.

" 'Cause Ma Fisher's birthin' cord stretches for miles to wherever her sons are," Geezer said. "She could be anywhere in the territory."

"Came into town to see about more time on my mortgage payment this month," Mallory said.

"You've got your extension, Mister Mallory," Rose said. "Now go on home and see to your family."

Mallory nodded, looking a little pale. He spun on his heels and made a hasty exit to the street, then untied his horse and mounted up. Slocum followed him out.

"Mallory," Slocum called.

Mallory turned in the saddle toward Slocum.

"Thanks again," Slocum said. "Hope to see you around."

"Likewise," Mallory called back. He spurred his horse and galloped off down Main Street.

Slocum went back into the jail, where Slug Fisher was slowly coming around, judging from the painful moans coming from his cell. Rose and Geezer were standing nearby, looking concerned. Even behind a locked cell door and semiconscious, he still looked meaner than a rabid coyote. An ugly jagged scar that could have only come from a broken whiskey bottle ran down his face from his left ear to his cheek. A fair-sized chunk of his right ear was missing, *and damn if it wasn't bit off*, Slocum thought, staring down in disgust at his new prisoner.

"Real prairie trash," he said to no one in particular.

Slocum grabbed a chair and sat outside the locked cell, then started leisurely reloading his Colt.

"Rose," Slocum said, "go into the empty cell, grab the blanket off the empty bunk."

"This is hardly a time to worry about his comfort," Rose said.

Slocum ignored her. To Geezer he said, "Lie down on the floor over there." He pointed to the space near the door.

"What the hell fer?" Geezer wanted to know.

"Just do it," Slocum snapped angrily. He knew he was neck-deep into it now, and the thought irritated him to no end. Less than twenty-four hours ago, his biggest worries were finding a place to get a bath and a shave, and maybe getting his hands on some female flesh.

Rose knew from the tone in Slocum's growl that questioning him would not be a prudent move, and she hastily tore the dirty blanket off the bunk. Geezer similarly followed Slocum's instructions, and stretched himself out on the cold stone floor of the jail.

"Cover his old hide with the blanket," Slocum said to Rose.

"Old hide?" Geezer said indignantly as Rose spread the blanket over him, covering his face. "I'll dance on your grave, you redneck peckerwood." His protests were muffled under the thick blanket.

"Just shut your craw and act like you're dead," Slocum snapped. He turned to Rose. "You best be going before he comes to," he said to her, motioning toward Slug, whose eyes were fluttering open now. "Best he don't see you at all."

Rose wisely saw the logic of Slocum's advice. She went to him and kissed him on the check.

"We appreciate your help, John," she said.

"It's my pleasure," he said. "Or it will be when you put me on salary."

"Save my town from the Fishers," she said, "and I'll make you a rich man."

"We'll talk about it," Slocum said.

Rose managed a small smile and pinched Slocum's cheek.

"Your mother did a good job, Slocum," she said. "Watch your ass." She turned and made a hasty exit.

Slocum watched her slink out the door and commented, "I'd rather watch yours."

"Anytime, anywhere," she said, throwing the door open and disappearing into the blazing morning sun.

Slocum turned to watch Slug Fisher fully regain consciousness. He shook the last of the cobwebs out of his head and focused his eyes on Slocum. He rubbed them to be double sure there were solid steel bars between him and the man calmly spinning the chamber of his gun.

"Where the hell am I?" Slug asked, sounding a little groggy. He tried to sit up and a red hot wave of pain crashed through the back of his head. "Damn," he croaked. He winced and patted the back of his skull, checking for blood.

Slocum holstered his gun and grabbed a stick of firewood next to the potbellied stove. He pulled out his pocketknife, flipped the blade, and started whittling as though he hadn't a care in the world.

"You're in a jail cell in Roseville, Texas," Slocum said.

Slug Fisher sat up on the bunk; the effort clearly caused him a good amount of pain.

"Where's my buddies?" Slug asked, dabbing blood from his head wound and wiping it on his pants.

"You want to send them a letter," Slocum said, scraping chunks of bark off the stick, "you better address it to the gophers, 'cause that's who's deliverin' their mail now."

Slug didn't seem too concerned about the loss of his friends. Instead, he looked Slocum squarely in the eye and said, "You know who I am?"

"Why don't you tell me?" Slocum said. He continued whittling.

"You ever heard of the Fisher gang?" Slug asked.

Slocum stopped whittling and looked thoughtfully at the ceiling. He shook his head. "Can't say as I have."

Slug stood up and gripped the bars on the cell. "Well, you're gonna, lawman," Slug hissed. "And sooner'n you think, if you don't let me outta here."

"You tryin' to scare me, boy?" Slocum asked.

"When my ma finds out I'm in your jail, she'll cut your pecker off and feed it to the dogs." Slug spit through the bars.

"Your ma, huh?" Slocum said, sounding amused. "You need your mama to save your sorry ass?"

"You just wait," Slug said and smiled. Most of his front teeth were either missing or the color of old tar. "My ma's gonna eat your guts for breakfast."

"But not before she sees your filthy carcass hangin' from our gallows," Slocum said.

"Hang me, shit," Slug said with an ugly sneer. "Ain't no law 'gainst havin' a quiet drink."

"No, there ain't," Slocum said, "but we do got a few against killin'."

"What the hell are you talkin' about?" Slug growled.

Slocum stopped whittling and pointed to Geezer's still form under the blanket. "Him," Slocum said. He rose and walked over to the covered lump in the corner. He lifted the corner of the blanket. Underneath, Geezer played his part to the hilt. His eyes were open; he even managed to make them looked glazed over.

Nice touch, Slocum thought as he pulled the blanket back over the old codger's head.

"You're under arrest for the murder of Geezer McDougall," Slocum said.

"I didn't kill that old goat," Slug cried, gripping the bars of his cell. "Someone conked me on the head before I could even draw my gun."

"Not accordin' to our witnesses," Slocum said, "who saw you squeeze off two shots and plug Geezer in the back. Hell, I got your gun right here." He pulled the six-shooter from his belt and flipped open the chamber. "Two shots fired, and both of 'em in Geezer's back." He snapped the chamber closed. "This *is* your gun, ain't it?"

"Yeah, it's mine," Slug said defiantly, "but I didn't shoot that old desert rat."

"That's for the undertaker to say for sure," Slocum said. "But facts tend to speak for their ownselves." He shoved Slug's gun back into his belt. "You believe in Jesus, son?"

Slug snarled, "What's it to you?"

"If you don't, you best start," Slocum said. " 'Cause you're gonna be joining him for Sunday dinner real soon."

"Ain't you funny," Slug snorted. "If I ain't back by sundown tomorrow, my ma and my brothers'll burn this town and slaughter everyone in it. You best let me out if you know what's good for you."

"Seems to me," Slocum said, pulling the fixings for a smoke from his shirt pocket, "your ma's going to come here either way, whether you show up or not. Oh no, Fisher," he went on, "you're going to stand trial and most likcly hang. Hell, be one less of your ilk to kill when they do come."

Slug said nothing, gripping the bars of the cell.

"Yup," Slocum said, rolling a smoke. He curled the ends and said, "My gut tells me you'll be swinging by noon tomorrow. Folks don't much cotton to your type, Fisher. You best say your prayers, boy." He held out the cigarette. "Smoke?"

Slug reached for the cigarette, but Slocum snatched it away. Slug's eyes were black dots of hate.

"Bad for your health," he said, and popped it into his mouth. "You scared of dying, boy?"

"No more'n you," Slug answered.

"Tragedy is," Slocum said, "it don't have to be this way."

Slug's eyes narrowed. "What you mean?"

"I got some sway with the people of this town," Slocum said. "You help me out here, I might be able to convince 'em to not hang you."

Slug looked interested. "Yeah?"

"I'd like to have a little chat with your ma," Slocum said, striking a match and lighting his smoke. "Where can I find her?"

"You think I'm a-gonna tell you such?" Slug said.

"You will if you want to live," Slocum said.

Slug spat on the floor and lay down on the bunk. "Go to hell," he said.

"Have it your own way, then," Slocum said, and stood up. He walked over to Geezer's inert form and lifted the sheet, then swatted imaginary flies away.

"Yup, dead as a doornail," Slocum said. He opened the door and stepped outside into the sunlight. Waiting for him was every business owner in Roseville—Hiram Quick; Arthur Stoon, the tall, black-suited mortician; Hal Bracken, the bald, bespectacled editor of the *Roseville Gazette* who also owned the blacksmith shop; and Alfred Drake, who owned Drake's Bakery. His pigtailed, ten-year-old daughter, little Debbie, hid behind her father. Rose was also there, though she didn't look as apprehensive as everyone else. She was peering into a looking glass clenched in her left hand and painting her lips with the other.

She finished making herself look beautiful, and tucked the looking glass between her breasts. She looked at Slocum and said, "So?"

"So he won't talk," Slocum said.

"This is bad, this is very bad," said the Reverend Edward Horton. "What are we going to do?"

"Relax, Reverend," Rose said, and looked at Slocum. "What now, John?"

"Now we build a gallows," Slocum said.

"We going to hang him?" Hiram Quick asked.

"Maybe," Slocum answered. "We'll see."

Slug Fisher was awakened at dawn the next day by the sounds of sawing and hammering. He threw off the blanket and went to the window of his jail cell. Outside, he could see the townspeople well into erecting a platform and gallows. Slug grabbed his neck and swallowed. Sometime during the night, Geezer's body had been removed. He wanted to believe he was dreaming; *the gallows had to be for someone else*, he thought, but he knew he was only lying to himself. There was no one in the other cell. He was sure the lawman had been bluffing about his appointment to dance on air. Now he wasn't so sure.

Slocum burst through the door carrying a tray and whistling happily.

"Breakfast is served, Mister Fisher," Slocum said. He put the tray down on the desk and grabbed the keys to the cell. Slug could smell the enticing aromas of fried eggs, a chicken-fried steak, and biscuits with gravy. A big pot of coffee sat next to a stack of buttered walnut flapjacks, all courtesy of the cafe.

"Sorry we couldn't ask you what you wanted for your last meal," Slocum said, "but we figured this would suffice. After all, it ain't polite to ask a man what's sleeping the last thing he wants to eat before he hangs."

Slocum opened the cell door and placed the meal down on a rickety chair. Slug, seeing the open door, predictably dived at Slocum, who merely stuck out a fist which connected solidly with Slug's chin. Slug fell back onto the bunk with an audible grunt.

"Get it while it's hot," Slocum said, "and while you're still alive."

Slug rubbed his chin. "Eat it yourself, asshole."

Slocum smiled. "Thank you kindly," he said, taking the tray and slamming the cell door shut. He sat at the desk and tore into the food, eating lustily and making contented noises. "Don't know what you're missing, son," Slocum added, and belched. He bit into a fried egg; runny yellow yolk splashed onto his chin. "Yessir, that Mister Drake can sure bake a sweet biscuit."

Slug watched Slocum devour the food, wiping his watering mouth a few times on his sleeve.

"Too bad y'all are off your feed," Slocum said, wiping the last of the eggs with a biscuit. "Won't get a last meal like this over to Walnut Springs, no sir."

The hammering and sawing continued. Slug went to the barred window and looked out.

"What fer you building that?" Slug asked, pointing out the window.

"Well, shoot, son," Slocum said, "buildin' it for you. Gonna be painting it in another hour. You got a favorite color?"

"I ain't kilt no one," Slug protested. "And what about that trial you said I wuz gonna get?"

"Held it whilst you were asleep," Slocum answered, pouring himself a nice hot cup of coffee.

"You did?" Slug asked nervously. "How'd I do?"

"Guilty as hell," Slocum said.

Slug grimaced.

"Come high noon," Slocum said, "you got an appointment with the business end of a rope."

Slug took another look out the window. The construction of the gallows was almost complete. Slocum lifted the tray and carried it out of the jail. Outside, Rose was waiting.

"How much longer do we have to keep up this charade?" she wanted to know. She was clutching a hammer and was wearing bib overalls, and looking like a million. Slocum guessed she'd look pretty in a circus tent.

"I told him he's to hang at noon," Slocum said. "By the time the church bells ring out eleven o'clock, he'll be sweating bullets. By half past he'll break like a dry twig."

"And then what?"

"He'll tell me what I want to know," Slocum said. "Perkey back yet?"

"Rode in ten minutes ago," Rose said. "Rode all night. Brought in some of the ranchers. The rest should be along soon. Some of them needed extra convincing, but they came. This is my town, John."

Slocum didn't question it. "Herd them into the church when they're all here. I want them all in one place, sober too."

Rose nodded, wondering what Slocum had up his sleeve. It would be exciting, whatever it was.

Slocum turned to leave, but Rose grabbed him and threw her arms around his neck and kissed him.

"Again, thanks for helping, John" she said.

"Help nothing," Slocum said. "This will cost you, Rose."

"How much?" she asked, placing a hand on her shapely hip.

"When this is all over," he answered, "you'll find out in spades."

"Something to look forward to," she said with a smile, and went back to helping the good people of Roseville build a gallows exclusively for the purpose of scaring a lowlife desperado named Slug Fisher.

At half past eleven that morning, Slocum sat at the jail house desk and munched a thick ham sandwich slobbered with mustard. He had yet to chow down on the big turkey leg or the huge slab of blueberry pie. A big mug of beer sat next to them on the desk. Slocum took a sip between bites of the sandwich.

Unlike breakfast, Slocum didn't offer any of the early dinner to Slug Fisher. He knew the vicious little toad would be famished by this time. Slug hadn't eaten since at least before midafternoon yesterday. He also knew that Slug was terrified of what the strike of twelve meant for the close relationship between his neck and everything that came below it. Fear, for reasons Slocum never really knew, sometimes made a man even hungrier. What Slocum did know was that the energy a man burned up being scared made him much more likely to cave in. Slug wasn't there quite yet. His brow was sparkling with beads of sweat and his knees, as he sat on the bed, knocked together so fast a man could chafe wheat between them.

"Lookin' a little pale, Slug," Slocum said, trying to savor the ham sandwich. His belly was still stuffed from breakfast, and each swallow wanted to turn around and come back up.

Slocum took a sip of beer. Slug watched, gripping the bars of the cell and licking his lips hungrily. Even Slocum could hear Slug's insides growling.

"Sure you don't want a little bite before you swing, Slug?" Slocum asked.

Slug's face contorted into a mask of hate and fury. He eyed the turkey leg, licking his stubbled chops.

Slocum chewed the sandwich slowly, deliberately, one eye cocked on Slug, who looked hungry enough to bite the head off a buffalo.

"Wouldn't mind that turkey leg," Slug rasped. "Iffen it's all the same to you."

"Matter of fact, it ain't," Slocum said, and managed to force down the rest of the ham sandwich. He grabbed the turkey leg and picked at it with his fingers. "I'm sorry, Slug," Slocum apologized. "How rude of me! Were you hungry?"

"A little," Slug answered, his eyes riveted to the turkey leg.

"Now I'm impressed," Slocum said fondly. "A man not wantin' to meet his Maker on an empty stomach. Shows you got *cojones*, son."

Slocum went to the cell and offered the turkey leg to Slug. Slug ripped it out of Slocum's fist and tore into it like a beaver to a branch. Slocum went and grabbed the mug of beer, and held it out. Slug grabbed it, took a big swallow, and then returned to the turkey leg, ripping off huge hunks of meat.

"Have some mustard," Slocum said. He grabbed the small crock on the tray and slapped some on the turkey leg.

Slocum turned and whistled. On cue, the jail door opened and a mangy old dog was pushed inside. It sniffed around for a second, then hobbled over to Slocum. Slug was ravenously biting off a hunk of meat when he saw that the dog was missing a back leg.

"Nice poochy," Slocum said, and picked up the smelly, shaggy mutt. "Name's Raider," Slocum said to Slug. "Nice dog—until he fell in with a gang of no-good, low-down mongrels and went where he shouldn't of been. Got his leg tore off." He rubbed the stub of the dog's missing back leg.

Slug stopped chewing and spit out the half-eaten meat. He looked at the turkey leg—which was just that—in horror, and flung it to the floor.

"You stinkin' bastard!" Slug thundered. He fell to his knees and started sobbing. "How many ways you fixin' on killin me?"

"None, Slug," Slocum said. "I gave you a choice: talk to me or die. Thus far you ain't done any talkin', so now you're gonna die. I figure that's fair."

"Ma would kill me iffen I tol' you where she was at," Slug said with his chest heaving.

"And I'll kill you if you don't," Slocum said. He pulled a stopwatch from his pocket, which he had borrowed from Hiram Quick for the occasion, and looked at it. "In fifteen minutes." He pocketed the watch and added, "Just see if I don't."

"An old ranch around here," Slug blurted out. "The old Cy Roberts place, that's what she said." Slug was paler than a fresh coat of white paint on a barn. "You really gonna hang me?"

Slocum grunted and shook his head. "Not that I wouldn't like to," he said, "but right now, you're this town's ace in the hole."

He went on outside, where Geezer, Perkey, and Rose were chattering at each other. Perkey was pointing to the scaffold, which was nearly finished. The townies had really pulled together during this crisis.

They turned to Slocum as he approached. "They're holed up at the old Cy Roberts place," Slocum said. "Anyone know where it is?"

"Dennis Mallory bought it last year," Perkey said.

Mallory was the kid who had backed Slocum up against Slug and his men. He'd ridden off the day before to see to his wife and baby daughter.

They were all thinking the same thing, but it was Geezer who said, "Man's riding straight into the eye of hell."

Slocum said, "Best saddle up the two fastest horses you got in town, Perkey. Maybe we can get to Mallory in time." In his heart, though, he didn't believe they could.

8

Slocum and Perkey lay flat on their stomachs at the top of a ridge a quarter-mile from the Mallory place. From their vantage point, through the mesquite and clumps of pecan trees, they had an unobstructed view of the sickening spectacle unfolding.

Ma was swigging corn liquor from a jug, roaring drunk, bellowing obscenities and egging her boys on to new heights of sadism. Her sons and the other vipers were running wild, drinking, shooting, and pillaging. They'd already burned the barn, which now was a smoldering black shell. Some were blasting the heads off chickens and baby hogs. Hank had wanted to kill the horses for sport, but Ma had stopped him. Couldn't hurt to have a few extra for their trek down to Mexico, she said.

Slocum gritted his teeth as Hank Fisher came out of the small ranch house pulling up his pants. Minutes earlier, Hank had dragged Mallory's young wife, Katie, inside to the accompaniment of her bloodcurdling screams. Then, two more men went inside, and the screams started anew. Slocum had never felt so helpless in his life.

Dennis Mallory appeared to be long dead. He was strapped to a fence post, riddled with red holes. Two men took turns blowing off what little was left of his head while passing a bottle back and forth. Their baby daughter, who couldn't have been more than two years old, sat in the trampled vegetable garden, bawling her little lungs out in terror.

"Sons of bitches," Perkey muttered. "Dirty low-down bastards."

"How many, you reckon?" Slocum asked Perkey. He already had a good idea.

"Ten, give or take," Perkey said. "What's with that crazy Jesus jumper?"

Perkey was pointing at Preacher, who was standing atop a wooden crate, bellowing and waving a Bible at the sky. He was totally ignored; the Fisher gang had better things to do.

"Got to be Preacher McCall," Slocum said, eyeing the skinny old buzzard with hatred. "Heard tell of him. Rode with Quantrill, raped and burned his way across Kansas. Just goes to show you," Slocum added, "the Lord works in mysterious ways."

"We could kill a bunch of 'em right now," Perkey said, "and still get away in one piece."

"Could at that," Slocum said, "but then the rest will slaughter Mallory's wife and kid."

"They'll do it anyways."

"That's what I'm afraid of," Slocum said, scrambling to his feet. "Cover me."

"Where the hell you think you're going?" Perkey asked.

"Don't imagine I'd ever sleep well at night if I didn't at least try to save Mallory's family."

"Gonna waltz in there all casual like and save

'em, that your plan?" Perkey asked with some acid.

"Something like that," Slocum answered. "With any luck, they'll all start passing out from too much strong drink."

Half an hour later, Slocum was crouched behind a cluster of brush, maybe two hundred yards from where the Mallory baby sat bawling. Her mother's anguished cries had trickled off as each man took his turn with her inside the house. The debauchery was definitely winding down as indicated by the gang members, who were starting to drop like drunken flies. A dozen or so buzzards circled the scene of the carnage, hovering like black angels of death.

Slocum had managed to make his way down the ridge and as close to the ranch house as he could without being detected. Ma Fisher was propped up against the house swigging from the jug with a little less enthusiasm now. In another minute, her eyelids would snap shut, and he could make his move. It was dusk, and Preacher McCall poked listlessly at a camp fire.

"Throw some more wood on that fire," Ma barked at Preacher, her words slurred. One last man staggered out of the house, his pants at his knees, and fell flat on his face. He started to snore contentedly.

Slocum waited a few more minutes until Ma passed out. The others had either done so or were in the process. He crept out silently from behind the clump of brush and crawled over to the baby girl, who had also quieted and was sucking her thumb. Slocum grabbed her from behind. She started to bawl again until he quickly clamped his hand over her mouth. Preacher McCall looked up suspiciously from the fire. Unlike the others, he hadn't indulged in the sins of the flesh, nor of the bottle. He'd forsworn both some years earlier. Nowadays, he took his pleasure in the Good Book and slaughtering disbelievers.

Slocum, holding the baby, darted back behind the brush with the stealth of a jackrabbit.

"You hush now, little one," Slocum whispered in her ear. Preacher caught only a glimpse of what he thought was one of the gang members taking the baby behind a bush for purposes he cared not to contemplate. The venal lusts of men sickened and angered him. To his way of thinking, it was a sin to spread a woman's legs but quite all right to blow her head off.

He'd snatch that baby from the cradle of hell and deliver it from sin, Preacher Horace McCall decided. Of course, he'd baptize it in the trough before slitting its little throat.

Preacher stomped over to the brush and peered behind it. Slocum was waiting, the baby clenched in his arm and his gun pointed at the surprised preacher.

"Open your mouth and you'll be shaking hands with your Maker," Slocum said, aiming at Preacher's head.

Preacher turned to call for Ma Fisher. Before he could, though, Slocum jumped up, still clutching the baby, and clocked Preacher on the skull with the butt of his gun. He crumpled at Slocum's spurs. Slocum gave him a firm kick in the head for good measure.

"Let's get your mama," Slocum said to the baby,

who then proceeded to soil her diapers. The aroma was anything but pleasant.

"Can't say as I blame you," Slocum said, tucking the baby neatly under his arm and creeping carefully toward the house. The Fisher gang was sprawled everywhere. One man was draped over the porch swing, another was passed out under it.

Slocum stole inside the house. A few candles cast faint shadows on the walls. In the corner, Katie Mallory lay moaning softly on the bed. Her face was purple and puffy; one eye was swollen shut. Her lips were crusted with dried blood. Hank and his fellow barbarians had done a fine job on her.

Slocum crouched beside the bed, his hand still clenched over the baby's mouth. "I'm John Slocum, a friend. We've got to go now, Missus Mallory," he whispered to her. "Can you stand?"

She opened her one good eye and saw Slocum clutching her daughter. "I think so," she said. Slocum curled his free arm around her waist and helped her unsteadily to her feet. Then he felt cool metal against the back of his head.

"Goin' somewhere?" asked the voice of an old lady from behind him.

"Kill me and you'll never see your son Slug again," Slocum said.

Slocum suddenly didn't feel the metal barrel of the gun against his head anymore. "Turn around," the old lady snapped.

Slocum turned, dragging Katie Mallory with him. The baby drooled against his chest. He came face to face with the one and only Charity "Ma" Fisher. She was even uglier up close. The wanted posters actually did her justice.

"Now what was that about my boy?" Ma asked, pointing the gun at Slocum's head.

"He's in the Roseville jail," Slocum said, "and they'll stretch his neck like warm taffy if I ain't back by dawn."

Ma studied Slocum for a moment. Her eyes bleary red from drink but still cunning and alert. "Boys!" she croaked. "Get your worthless asses in here!"

Outside, he could hear the Fisher brood coming around groggily. They dutifully started filing into the house, Bo, Little Bo, Mortimer, and Hank, like participants in an ugly contest. Each pointed his gun at Slocum.

"Who are you?" Ma wanted to know. "You got balls comin' in here."

"John Slocum," he said, "and I'm leaving with this woman and this baby. That is, if you want to see your son again."

"How do I know you got him?" Ma asked.

Slocum leaned an unsteady Katie Mallory against the wall, then pulled a red polka dot handkerchief, the one he'd taken from Slug before leaving, from his back pocket. "Recognize this?"

Ma did, Slocum could see. "How do I know he ain't already dead?" she asked.

"You don't," Slocum said. "You in a gamblin' mood?"

"Guess I got no choice," Ma growled, then motioned to Little Bo, who was closest. She pointed to Katie Mallory. Little Bo grabbed the back of her torn dress and hauled her over. She swam in and out of consciousness, her head down, chin on chest.

Ma Fisher grabbed a handful of Katie Mallory's hair and jerked her head up. Ma stuck the barrel of her gun in Katie's ear and cocked the trigger.

"I'll ask you only once," Ma said slowly. "Is my boy still alive?"

"Yes," Slocum said, clutching the baby tightly.

Ma Fisher squeezed the trigger. A deafening roar filled the house as Katie Mallory's brain decorated Little Bo's face and chest. He didn't even flinch; his dazed smile was frozen on his face. Katie's lifeless body hit the floor like a sack of watermelons.

"I don't believe you," Ma Fisher said, turning her gun back on Slocum.

"You're a goddamned animal," Slocum couldn't help but mutter.

"This is my good side," Ma barked. "My son ain't alive, you'll see my bad."

"I'll keep it in mind," Slocum said softly, his eyes never leaving hers. "I'll be leaving now."

Slocum gingerly stepped around Katie Mallory's corpse as he walked toward the door. Nobody made a move to stop him. Slocum knew Ma wouldn't let them. His big hand pressed the baby's face against his chest.

He walked out of the house and toward the ridge where Perkey was waiting, half expecting a shot to be fired and the hot pain of a bullet slicing through his back.

None came. He walked straight ahead clutching the baby to him, not daring to look back. As he stepped through the vegetable patch he heard Ma call out, "Hey, Slocum!"

Slocum stopped and slowly turned back to the house. Ma was standing in the doorway, her stocky form silhouetted in the dim candlelight.

"I'll see you in hell," she said to him.

Slocum held the baby even tighter.

"I'll be waiting," he said.

At roughly the same time, Rose and Mayor Hiram Quick stood on the pulpit of the church and attempted to take control of the meeting. Every rancher in the territory—or that part of it affected by the Fishers' untimely visit—was assembled. They were talking heatedly among themselves, sometimes yelling, and passing a few bottles of whiskey. This did not go unnoticed by the good Reverend Edward Horton, who wrinkled his nose in distaste. Still, he knew better than to ask them to cease. These ranchers were a rowdy bunch; Jimmy Nash, one fateful Sunday morning when he finally took Jesus into his heart, blew a big hole in the ceiling of the church in his frenzied religious fervor. Instead of chastising them, Reverend Horton sat behind Rose and Hiram Quick and kept his opinions to himself. The town had bigger problems than a few bottles of firewater.

The ranchers had been hastily called into town to volunteer their services against the notorious Fisher bunch. The word spread quickly through the territory, starting at Mike Bannon's Bar B. Since the word had come directly from Rose via Perkey, the ranchers didn't hesitate. It didn't hurt that Rose owned the bank and held the notes on virtually all of their spreads. Only Norval Jones of the Lazy G, who was as blind as a bat and missing his left leg to boot, wasn't indebted to the Roseville Savings and Loan, having settled the land thirty years earlier. His blindness was an act of nature; his missing leg was an act of a Confederate cannonball. Now, he waved his crutch wildly and raved about the devil's horde smacking them in their heads.

Rose screamed for quiet, then whistled shrilly with two fingers, a little trick acquired on the streets of the Lower East Side. Hiram Quick, mayor in name only, winced. Rose ran the show in Roseville, but was smart enough to know that men weren't clever enough—nor would their egos allow them—to take orders from a woman. Now, though, she knew that cool heads needed to prevail, and no man in Roseville at this moment could boast of having one.

"Shaddup!" Rose bellowed at the top of her lungs. The ranchers fell silent—out of shock, not out of respect.

Rose surveyed the room. "Better," she said. "Now sit the hell down."

Grumbling, the ranchers did just that.

"Now as you all know," she said, "we got trouble, right here in Roseville."

"Trouble with a capital T!" Hiram Quick put in his two cents' worth with a glint of satisfaction. He loved it when he got to yell at the unruly ranchers and get away with it.

Rose ignored him. "The Fisher gang is most likely on their way to our town, and I don't think I need to mention what they're capable of."

"Shoot the bastards where they stand," Norval Jones called out, "and leave their rottin' hides for the ants to get sick on! Back when I first come here, we killed the Comanche and didn't set around jawin' about it first."

"Thank you, Norval," Rose said patiently. "If we could—"

"Cut out their gizzards and mounted 'em on

sticks," Norval Jones cried. "After them Comanche were the Meskins. Blowed their butts off, too. One time—"

"Quiet, Norval!" Geezer snapped from the front pew. "Let the woman speak, ya old fool!"

"*Old fool?*" Norval yelled, rising to his foot angrily, forgetting, as he always did, to use his crutch. He usually got two-thirds of the way up before toppling back again. "Why, you booze hound old bastard—"

"Shaddup!" Rose bellowed again. "Save your energy for the Fishers, for the love of God."

"Amen," Reverend Horton squeaked.

"I just got one question for you boys," Rose said. "Who's going to help defend this town, and who isn't? All those who are, stand now. All those who aren't, don't stand."

The ranchers, knowing this was coming, looked at each other apprehensively and shifted nervously.

Rose shot a look at Geezer, who nodded and stood.

"At least we have one man here," Rose said. She asked Charlie Russell of the Bar C, "How many hands you got working for you, Charlie?"

"Three, all told," Charlie said.

"And you, Norval," Rose said. "How many you got?"

"My sons Egbert and Donald," the blind rancher replied.

Rose turned to look at Jonah Wilbershot of the Bar W. "I know you got two men working as well, Jonah," Rose said. "That's more than fifteen. More than enough to stand up to the Fishers."

"You're forgettin' one thing, Miss Rose," Charlie Russell said. He was a tall man with a big gut that looked out of place on his frame. "Them Fishers is ambidextrous, and that's twice as many guns."

"That's right," Owen Grey of the Bar G piped up, "and our hands are cowpunchers, not gunfighters. Even if they was, they ain't a-gonna risk their lives for no ten dollars a month."

The other ranchers murmured in agreement. None seemed eager to throw in their lot in a war they couldn't possibly win. The Fishers could shoot like lightning while most of them were slow as rain.

"I'll double it," Rose said. "Better still, I'll offer twenty-five dollars to any man who takes up arms against the Fishers. Fifty dollars a kill—cash."

"Mighty tempting, Miss Rose," said Abel Gormly of the Gormly Ranch, "but you ain't got enough money in your bank to pay for a human life."

Rose stiffened.

"That's what you're askin', and for a lousy twenty-five dollars," Gormly said. "I cain't ask my help to defend a town that they ain't got no stake in. They'd sooner kill *me*."

"So forget your help," Rose said. "I'll go back to my original question. Who here is going to fight for this territory?"

There were no takers except for one-legged Norval Jones, who struggled to stand again, this time using his crutch for support.

"I was hoping I wouldn't have to bring this up," Rose said, "but let's not forget who's holding the notes on your spreads." She paused, scanning the rows of ranchers. "I'm in a position to call in each and every one of them." Her eyes were hard, "and it wouldn't make a dent in my pocketbook."

Owen Grey stood, hat in hand, curling the brim anxiously.

"We all know you got us by the short hairs, Miss Rose," Grey said, "but you're askin' one hell of a lot—to maybe get dead for a few lousy buildings. All the Fishers want is whiskey, women, and maybe the few dollars they can rob from the bank. Then they'll go on their way."

"Tell that to Dennis Mallory," Rose said. "The Fishers more than likely slaughtered his family by now. Could have been any of you."

"All the more reason to stay out of it," Grey said. "From here they'll head straight to Mexico, and none of us are in their path."

"That's right," Charlie Russell said. "We lay low and we'll come through just fine."

"Then have it your own way," Rose said coldly. "But remember one thing: you all fought to tame this land, and now you have to fight to keep it tamed. You don't make a stand now, and you'll be opening the door to every piece of lowlife prairie scum looking to tear himself off a piece of your living."

"Ain't nothing worth dying for," Russell murmured. "Not a few head of cattle and a house that blows down every time a twister comes off the panhandle."

Rose looked at them, sighing. They were tired, middle-aged men who'd been trying to work a harsh land for too many years. They had neither the energy nor the enthusiasm for killing. Their pipes and porch swings never looked better.

"Help me," Rose said, "and I'll burn the notes I'm holding on your spreads." She added sourly, "That's my best offer."

"If we refuse, then what?" Owen Grey said.

Rose, her face ashen, stepped off the pulpit and walked slowly to the church door. She suddenly looked older, like a woman who knew the worst was yet to come. The ranchers felt sorry for her, but continued to stare down at their boots all the same.

"Then nothing," Rose said, looking like a wounded puppy. A plump tear rolled down her cheek. It was enough to make the sturdiest of the ranchers feel lower than a snake's toes. "I used to have high hopes for this territory and its people. Guess I was only fooling myself."

She blew her nose into a lace hanky and said, "But I understand."

She made a dramatic exit and slammed the door behind her. Hiram Quick blinked uncomfortably at Reverend Horton, who also looked extremely sad. He stood and walked to the door. Hiram Quick followed him. Reverend Horton pushed the door open and turned to face the ranchers.

"Time was," Reverend Horton said, "when I tried to get you into my church. Now though, I'd just as soon see you all leave." He held the door open for them.

Slowly the ranchers got up and filed sullenly out of the church. Even Norval Jones limped on out dejectedly. Rose, hiding behind the back wall of the church watched them shuffle listlessly into the street. Reverend Horton whistled softly, and Rose poked her head out from behind the church wall. She saw the ranchers head for one of the saloons, then she crept back through the church doors. Reverend Horton closed it hastily. Only Geezer remained.

"What do you think?" Reverend Horton asked her.

"Maybe they'll come through, maybe they won't," Rose said, watching them disappear into the saloon to splash down enough whiskey to wash away the pain of their cowardice. But there wasn't that much booze, Rose knew, in the whole territory.

9

Perkey had the horses waiting, gripping the reins, as Slocum came scurrying up over the ridge, clutching the baby firmly against his chest. Sweat dripped off his face.

Ma and her gang had thus far not chosen to pursue Slocum, though he would have been an easy target. She was, fortunately, taking his threat seriously. For now, anyway.

"Saddle up, Perkey," Slocum snapped. Perkey climbed onto his roan and grabbed the baby from Slocum as he mounted his own horse.

"In all my born days," Perkey said, "I never met a body as blessed as your ownself. Figured you were a dead man for sure."

Slocum took the baby from Perkey and plopped the infant down on the saddle in front of him. He wrapped an arm around her. She looked a lot like her dear, departed mother, he thought quickly as he reined the horse around. He and Perkey took off at a brisk trot. Slocum, with the memory of Katie Mallory's brains splattering on the wall of the

113

ranch house still fresh in his mind, decided there and then that however long it took—the rest of his life if necessary—he would track Ma Fisher and her boys through darkest Africa or the frozen wastes of Antarctica and kill them one and all.

They hadn't gone more than half a mile or so before Slocum saw that Ma and her boys were in hot pursuit, and making excellent progress.

Both Slocum and Perkey spurred their horses faster and made a run for it. The baby started bawling again; she clearly didn't like being bounced around so. The cloud of dust coming up behind them signaled that the Fisher gang was gaining considerably. Not long after, shots started echoing in the distance. Even piss-drunk, these boys were pretty good shots.

"Didn't you tell Ma Fisher you'd hang her worthless son if she chased us?" Perkey wanted to know as they galloped east toward Roseville.

"Yeah," Slocum said, "but I sorta get the impression she ain't big on motherly love."

They rode harder and faster, but they knew it was just a matter of minutes before the Fishers would get the drop on them. "Guess we best make a stand of it," Perkey hollered over the pounding of hooves.

Slocum didn't need convincing. The Fishers were full of beans and hungry for fresh kills. Bullets zinged and clouds of dust exploded barely fifty feet behind them.

They headed for the dubious protection of a thick clump of mesquite trees on a rocky rise. Slocum heard a shot ring out that sounded especially close, then from the corner of his eye he saw Perkey's horse falter and then collapse into the rocky west Texas soil.

The Fishers were almost close enough to kiss. Perkey's horse lay dying as the lawman scrambled to his feet and ran for cover behind the mesquite.

Slocum, still clutching the baby, reined up behind the ridge and jumped from his horse, grabbing his Colt with his free hand. He aimed, drawing a bead on one of the Fishers, then realized he was toting an infant. Baby Mallory sucked a couple of fingers, looking wide-eyed in a curious sort of way.

Slocum dropped to his knees and leapfrogged behind the clump of mesquite with Baby Mallory under one arm. Breathing hard, the aroma of fresh baby shit suddenly assaulted his nostrils. Slocum gagged and kept moving. He deposited the baby safely between two rocks and, as an afterthought, placed his hat on the baby's belly. The hat covered most of the little rug rat.

"Chew on this," Slocum said, "and try not to crap again."

The baby gurgled happily and clutched Slocum's hat, fascinated by the new toy. She immediately started gnawing toothlessly on it.

Slocum lay flat against the side of the ridge and aimed again. Perkey was almost to the top of the ridge when more shots, closer this time, rang out and echoed in the breeze. Slocum saw blood burst from Perkey's gut and the lawman fell to the ground with an audible grunt. He clamped a hand over his belly and crawled over to Slocum. Blood oozed from the gaping hole in Perkey's belly. The lawman fought off the approaching shock, the color already draining from his usually ruddy face. The wound was bad and, they both knew, more than likely fatal, as gut shots were.

"Shit," Perkey grunted. He drew his pistol and started firing at the enemy, who were fast approaching and would soon be able to surround the ridge, leaving Slocum and Perkey open to a massacre. Their best bet was to kill as many of Ma Fisher's boys as they could before that could happen.

"Get the one on the far left," Slocum said to Perkey, "and I'll drill the one on the far right. Maybe we can—"

"Screw that," Perkey said, his strength ebbing with each syllable. "Make a run for it, Slocum. I can hold 'em off."

"The hell you say," Slocum said, squeezing off a shot and missing a rider by a good five yards. "We won't get fifty feet."

A red patch was growing larger and wider on Perkey's white shirt, spreading like wildfire.

"You stick around and we're both finished," Perkey said, his breathing labored now. "You saved my hide once, not it's time for me to return the debt."

"I ain't leavin' without you, Perkey, so shut your trap." Slocum squeezed off another shot, this time blowing off a substantial chunk of a rider's head. The rider pitched forward on his horse and was dead before he hit the ground. In the meantime, bullets whizzed all around them, kicking up dust inches from them. Nearby, Baby Mallory chewed contentedly on Slocum's hat.

"Come on, you fool," Perkey said, and coughed blood. "I'm done for. We both know it, so take the kid and make a run for your horse." Perkey coughed up more blood. "Don't be a *schmuck*, Slocum."

"*Schmuck!*" Slocum said. "You been hangin' around Rose Liebowitz too long, friend."

"Whatever," Perkey said, weakening and coughing harder. Blood gurgled through his clenched teeth. "I still got a few minutes before I meet my Maker." Then he added softly, "Go now, John, while you can. It's your only chance. Don't worry—I'll be dying the way I was meant to, with my boots on." Perkey coughed again. "Though never could figure out why that was so damned important."

"Me neither," Slocum said, and slithered over toward the baby. He grabbed her and retrieved his hat. Jamming it onto his head, he started crawling like a snake through the brush toward his roan, who was grazing unperturbed on prairie grass nearby. The sounds of gunshots didn't phase him anymore; not John Slocum's steed.

"I'll come back for you, Perkey," Slocum said, taking one last look back.

"Then you best bring along a shovel," Perkey said, and turned to face the enemy for the last time. "Just do me one favor. Keep an eye on Roseville for me."

"Deal," Slocum said, starting to move again.

"I'm obliged," Perkey said, firing one last shot, but Slocum was already gone.

Slocum mounted with the baby still tucked under his arm, and spurred the roan. He galloped off a minute before Ma Fisher and her boys surrounded the late lawman. His luck was holding; Ma and her boys obviously didn't know that Slocum had made good his escape.

Slocum spurred the faithful roan harder. Behind him he could hear more shots. He rode to the top of a hill and, figuring he was far enough away, reined the roan to a stop and looked back.

The Fishers had dismounted and were circling around Perkey, who was either dead or doing an excellent imitation. Nonetheless, the Fishers circled him like hungry cats around a paralyzed sparrow.

Slocum could faintly hear angry voices. Then Ma Fisher and some of her boys fired at Perkey's lifeless form, spitting at least twenty bullets into him.

Slocum saw Ma Fisher stomp away and start firing angrily at the sky, the setting sun silhouetting her large figure.

"I know you're out there, Slocum!" she bellowed into the dusk. The sound of her whiskey-hoarse, savage screams sent a flock of quail fluttering up out of the brush. "You hurt one hair on my boy's head and you'll be shitting out of eight holes instead'a one!"

"We'll just see," Slocum murmured to himself. He clutched the baby more firmly and spurred the roan forward.

10

Slocum sat at a table in the cafe and devoured a bowl of greasy stew, ripping off chunks of a half-stale loaf of bread and wiping up the gravy. He slurped and swallowed a lukewarm beer.

"Poor Perkey," Rose said sadly, a lace hankie clenched in her tense hands. She sat opposite Slocum at the table, a cup of cold coffee in front of her. "Can't even give him a decent burial."

"The Mallorys didn't fare so well, neither," Slocum said, polishing off the stew. In spite of everything that was happening, he was still hungry. Fighting and narrow escapes always had that effect on him.

"Any chance of gettin' more stew?" he asked.

"Amelia," Rose called out, and the half-wit woman came doddering out of the kitchen. "More stew for Mister Slocum."

"If the first servin' didn't kill him, don't reckon another will." Amelia grabbed the bowl and disappeared back into the kitchen.

"What about the kid?" Slocum asked. He had

handed Baby Mallory over to Martha Phipps, the wife of the old town sawbones, Doc Phipps.

"She's fine," Rose said. "Martha Phipps is tending to her."

"I sort of expected to see some of the local ranchers in town by now," Slocum said.

"Forget them, John," Rose said. "Nothing but a bunch of cowardly, yellow-bellied *schlemiels*. Not one of them stood up to defend their town."

"It ain't their town, Rose," Slocum said. "It's yours." He tore off a chunk of bread. "Slug give you any grief while I was gone?"

"Cried himself to sleep a couple of hours ago," Rose said. "No problems."

"They're comin' for him, Rose," Slocum said, "and they'll destroy everything in their path. We ride out now, this minute, we'll make it."

Rose's eyes were like shining blue sapphires. "Like you said, Slocum, this is my town. I built one half, and the other I financed. There was nothing but an outhouse of a saloon, a broken down trading post, and a lot of rattlesnakes when I landed here." She waved an angry finger in his face. "And I'm not about to let a band of cutthroats run me out." Her cheeks flushed fire-red. "If you think for one minute that I would—"

"Sweet Jesus," Slocum hissed, shaking his head. "You sure do rile easy, woman." He tilted back in his chair, bootheels scraping the floor, his spurs jingling. "Relax, have a drink or something. It was just a suggestion."

"Well, it stinks," Rose said, sitting back down as Amelia brought out Slocum's seconds of stew. She placed it on the table in front of him with a palsied hand and managed to slop half of it into his lap.

Slocum jumped up with a howl and brushed the steaming stew off his crotch with a napkin as the old woman shuffled back to the kitchen.

"Thank you, Amelia," Rose said with a small smile.

Slocum sank wearily to his chair, then balled up his napkin and tossed it into the remains of the stew, but he still had enough energy to glare at Rose.

"Don't get mad at me," she said. "I didn't burn your balls."

"I got half a mind—"

"I agree," Rose said.

"—to ride out of here right now. I had my ass shot off, saved some baby from bein' used as target practice, and watched a good lawman get ventilated. And you know what?" he asked. "I ain't seen a dime for my troubles. You want me to stick around, it'll cost you." He leaned closer to the table and looked Rose squarely in the eye. "Time is money," he said. "And so is blood."

"So what are you telling me, Slocum?" Rose asked. "That time is blood?"

"No." Slocum snorted impatiently. "That blood is time . . . that money is blood, no, that blood is money . . . that—" He swept the bowl of stew and the tarnished silverware off the table and jumped from his seat. He pulled off his hat and wiped his brow. Somehow, he always sweated more when he was around Rose Liebowitz. She was the only woman who had this effect on him, and Slocum hated it.

"Goddamit, woman!" Slocum sputtered. "You got

a rare gift for gettin' a man all flustered up."

"You want to talk about money, John," Rose said evenly, "then let's talk about money."

"It's about time," Slocum said.

"Help me," she said. "I'll give you a piece of everything I've got."

"A piece of what, exactly?" Slocum wanted to know.

"A piece of the bank, the hotel, saloons, the cafe, and the dress shop, and the newspaper, and the livery and half the ranches in the territory. I also have a herd of blooded stock, fifteen thousand head, down around Corpus Christi. I have investments in salmon canneries in Seattle, and horse-trading companies in El Paso, and whorehouses from San Angelo to Abilene. Without going into details, my estimated worth totals over a million dollars."

Slocum tried not to gasp and instead kept a poker face.

"Only a million?" he asked.

"Probably more," she said. "I'll triple it in three years. I'd like to have someone around to share it with. I like to think it might be you."

"It could," Slocum said. "Bein' with you's sort of been in the back of my mind."

"So what do you say, Slocum?" Rose asked. "Are you and me going to be one, or what?"

"It's possible," Slocum said. "Let's save your town and then talk about it."

He went to her, grabbed her arm, and dragged Rose to her feet. He threw his arms around her, pulling her close. He tried to kiss her, but Rose turned away.

"Sorry, Slocum," she said, breaking away from

him. "But I close a deal with a handshake, not a kiss."

Slocum said, "Then maybe I will move on," then turned to leave. Rose grabbed his arm this time and pulled him back against her.

"You do and I'll kill you," she said, and kissed him.

"Then I guess I got nothing to lose," Slocum said.

"Way I got it figured," Slocum told the ranchers and some of the townspeople in the saloon, "the Fishers'll be riding into town a little after sunup. Six hours, give or take, unless Ma decides to try for her boy a little sooner. Not likely, though; I'm told rapin' and murderin' and drinkin' yourself into a stupor takes a lot out of a body." He paused for effect, then added, "You all remember the Mallorys, your friends and neighbors."

There were a few grunts and coughs from the ranchers.

"My guess is," Slocum went on, "that they'll make camp for the night. Ma knows we won't hurt her baby boy, Slug—he's the only reason for them snakes to leave their lair and get out in the open. Killin' Perkey was just her way of rubbin' it in our faces.

"The man died defending your butts, gentlemen," Slocum went on, helping himself to a glass of whiskey from Norval Jones's bottle.

"And was well paid fer it," Abel Gormly piped up, and immediately regretted it.

Slocum glared down at him.

"And what do *you* charge for dyin', mister?" Slocum said. Gormly, not the largest of men, immediately shrank back into himself like a dirty sock after too much starch.

"We got families to think of," said Jonah Wilbershot, "and we ain't no use to 'em dead."

"Then do what you got to do," Slocum said. "I'll defend Roseville, and not 'cause I got a stake in it, neither."

"Ain't what we heared," Mike Bannon commented from a back table, looking directly at Rose, who was standing behind the bar pouring herself a sarsaparilla.

Rose slammed the whiskey bottle down onto the mahogany bar. Even the toughest of the ranchers flinched. "And just what the hell is that supposed to mean, Michael Bannon?" Rose roared, her cheeks flushed so pink that even the darkest face powder couldn't hide it.

"Didn't mean no offense, Miss Rose," Bannon said.

"If you didn't mean no offense, Bannon," Slocum said, "you wouldn't of said it." He poured himself another shot, this time from Bannon's bottle. The stout rancher didn't protest. "Let me tell you something," he added, and pointed to Rose. "This woman's got more balls than all of you lily-livered weasels put together."

Rose looked at Slocum, her eyes wide. He'd just insulted every rancher in town, but not one of them challenged him. He had them cowed. His animal fury excited her.

"Rose Liebowitz," Slocum yelled, "has given her life's blood to the survival of this town. She fought, sweated, and sacrificed; she dared to build a piece of civilization in some of the hardest land in these

United States. She put her well-earned money into the future of every man in this saloon. So go, if you're of a mind to, but we can't promise there's going to be any town to come back to."

"You're askin' us to die for hardly anything, a few businesses—not to mention a bank that's holdin' notes on all of us to boot," Jonah Wilbershot said.

"And I'm callin' each and every one of them in right now," Rose blurted out, and walked over to where Jonah was sitting. "I've had it up to here. You owe the bank nearly two thousand dollars, Jonah." She spun around to Mike Bannon. "And you, Mike, owe me almost as much for those five hundred head and your ranch house."

Rose poured herself a big shot of Wilbershot's whiskey and gulped it down as Slocum had done. Unlike Slocum, though, she remembered she hated whiskey, and coughed, choked, and sputtered. Slocum felt a stab of love for her, even with the whiskey streaming out of her nose.

"There's not a-one of you who isn't late on your payments," she went on. "Hell, some of you are three, four months behind, and that gives me every right to foreclose here and now. What the hell—if you're not prepared to fight for your homes, then you don't deserve the privilege of owning them. If you can't pay, then I'll expect you all to vacate within twenty-four hours."

"That's right cold, Miss Rose," said Mike Bannon. "You know we're all good for it."

"Right now," she snapped back, "you're not good for much of anything."

She turned to Slocum. "I guess you were right, John. Let's hitch up a wagon with some supplies.

I'll clean out everything in the bank and we'll move on. I hear Amarillo has a lot of possibilities."

She walked slowly to the swinging saloon doors, not waiting for Slocum to follow, then turned back to the ranchers.

"I didn't invite Ma Fisher here, just remember that," she said. "And when you're run off your spreads by that bunch of murdering bastards, when you can't get a bolt of cloth for your missus, or a sack of flour, or a penny candy for your little ones because they burned the mercantile to the ground, when there's nowhere to buy a drink, or to get a haircut and shave, or worship under the hands of the Lord, when it all turns to deep, dark shit, don't cry your tears at my door."

She pushed through the swinging doors, then came right back in and scowled at Slocum. She crossed her arms impatiently and snapped, "You coming or what?"

"Yeah," Slocum said. "No reason to hang around here."

He followed her out into the street. Rose headed straight for the bank. The town was unusually quiet, since many people had already cleared out. Word of the Fishers' impending arrival plus the ranchers' reluctance to do something about it signaled a mass exodus. Hiram Quick was the first to light out, the cowardly piece of dirt. Quick's hasty departure opened the floodgates; after he left, so did just about everyone else. Oddly, though, Reverend Horton did not; he had retreated into the sanctity of his church. "The Fishers would never slaughter a man of God," was his reasoning, to which Rose had replied, "Don't be so sure, Edward." Nonetheless, Horton had decided to tough it out. Slocum, when he heard, admired the man more for it.

An hour later, Slocum had hitched a team of horses to a wagon that contained every last article of clothing and just about every personal item Rose owned—from perfume to the goose down mattress she'd slept on. Rose sat rigidly as Slocum hoisted one last suitcase onto the back. It weighed a ton.

"What do you got in here, anvils?"

"Money," she said. "A lot of it."

"Great," Slocum muttered. Large amounts of cash tended to bring out the worst in people, and it was anyone's guess who they might run into along the way to Amarillo, lowdown varmint-wise.

Geezer had, unlike Reverend Horton, accepted Rose's invitation to come along and was now snoring peacefully on Rose's goose down.

"Who knows," she said, more to herself, "maybe I'll go back East, to New York. Hell, even the Lower East Side is cakewalk compared to Texas."

"Horseshit," Slocum said, climbing onto the wagon and grabbing the reins. "You love Texas, else you wouldn't of stayed this long. Can't say as I blame you. Once this territory gets in your blood, it's hard to get out."

"Quit popping your bill and let's get a move on," she said irritably. Slocum smiled ruefully—there was something comical about hearing a well-worn Western phrase with a New York accent.

Slocum snapped the reins and they lurched off down Main Street. As they reached the outskirts of town, Rose took one look back and wiped a tear from her eye.

"Two years, maybe three, this could have been one hell of a town," she said wistfully. "If only the railroad had come through sooner, we could have afforded enough lawmen . . . if only—"

" 'If ifs and buts were candy and nuts, oh what a party we'd have,' " Slocum said. "My mama used to say that."

"Your mother was wonderfully wise," Rose said dryly.

They rode in silence for a mile or so out of town. Rose stared straight ahead, her expression grim. Geezer's snoring drowned out the creaking of the wagon wheels.

Suddenly, Rose grabbed Slocum's wrist as he reined the horses around a bend in the road.

"Stop," she said. "Stop now!"

"I told you to take care of that before we left," Slocum said.

"It ain't that, *schlemiel*," Rose snapped as Slocum jerked the reins back and halted the wagon. Rose jumped down and started pacing back and forth on the dry road, kicking up some dust.

"I never ran from a fight in my life," she said, rummaging through her velvet bag and producing an imported English cigarette. She popped it in her mouth, then pulled out a wooden match and struck it against the side of the wagon. She lit up and inhaled deeply, blowing out a thick stream of smoke. "Even back in Little Rock, when the Jesus-jumping church ladies tried to run me out of town, I stood firm and spat in their eyes." She waved an accusing cigarette at Slocum then puffed deeply again. "Then again in Brushwood Gulch, Colorado, when a bunch of fat jealous town ladies tried to have my house shut down and my girls tarred and feathered. Sure, I spread the cash around like manure on a tomato patch and bought my way out of it, but I didn't turn and run. I stayed, and I fought, and I triumphed."

She dropped the half-smoked cigarette on the ground and rubbed it out angrily with the heel of her boot. "For two thousand years my people have been persecuted, and sometimes I think that the worst is yet to come." She climbed back onto the seat of the wagon beside Slocum and added, "But not here, not now, and not me. I'm not going to let a band of wild animals chase me away and take what's mine." She turned to Slocum and grabbed his face, her fingertips firm on his cheeks.

"You turn this wagon around, Slocum," she said. She pulled Slocum's six-shooter from his holster and attempted to twirl it, but failed miserably. "Can you show me how to use this thing better?"

Slocum shook his head and snapped the reins, steering the horses around in a circle so that the wagon headed back the way it had come.

"Yeah," he said, "but the truth be told, I'm afraid to."

"And why is that?"

" 'Cause I get a bad feeling. If you can handle a gun the way you can handle everything else, God help us one and all," he said.

"You're probably right," she admitted.

An hour later, as they rolled back into town, they were greeted by a sight that brought a wide smile to Rose's lips.

There, standing in the middle of Main Street, lined up shoulder to shoulder and armed to the teeth, were the ranchers of Roseville, Texas, waiting to do battle with the forces of evil.

Slocum jerked the wagon to a stop in the middle of Main Street. Jonah Wilbershot stepped forward and said to the ranchers, "Gennelmen, I give you the ballsiest leader since Stonewall Jackson."

"We all had a hunch you'd be back, Miss Rose," Abel Gormly said, holding a Winchester.

"We did some studying on it," Mike Bannon added, "and all agreed you was right."

"And what do you intend to do about it?" Rose asked.

"Blow their butts back to hell," Norval Jones piped up. There were cries of agreement from the rest of the ranchers.

"Then let's get to work," she said, and turned in the seat to Slocum. "Got any ideas, John?"

Slocum didn't respond right off. Then he said to Rose, "Give me one of them fancy cigarettes."

She did. It was the first prerolled smoke he'd had in more years than he cared to remember. Rose struck a light for him.

Slocum smoked and thought about the Fisher gang. After the slayings of Perkey and the Mallorys—and Lord only knows how many others—he wanted them dead more than anyone else. Dennis Mallory had saved Slocum's life, as had Chester Perkey. *Vengeance is mine, sayeth the Lord*, Slocum mused, but screw Him. Slocum wanted to tear off a nice, big hunk for himself. Let the Lord fight His own fight. For starters, he wanted the pleasure of personally firing the bullet between Ma Fisher's cold, beady eyes. The world would definitely be a better placc without them, he was convinced. Sometimes it was necessary to spill a little blood to save a lot more.

"What's on your mind, John?" Rose asked casually. "You got a plan?"

"Yeah," Slocum said finally, "but it's a surprise."

"I hate surprises," Rose protested.

"You'll like this one," was all Slocum said as he climbed off the wagon and headed into the saloon.

"I do love that man," Rose murmured, and scrambled off the wagon to pour him a nice drink.

11

Hank Fisher nervously loaded his gun. Across the table, Ma sat and poured herself another glass of rotgut from a jug. Little Bo sat to her left, whittling a twig. In the corner by the fireplace, Preacher was muttering to himself from the Good Book.

It was a little after dawn. Hank was eager to saddle up and ride into Roseville and start blasting anything that had the nerve to move.

"What the hell are we waiting for?" Hank asked angrily, and spat into the fire. "Let's get a move on."

"That's just what we ain't gonna do, you dumbhead," Ma croaked, and poured herself another eye-opener from the jug. "No, we're gonna let 'em stew for a spell, say 'til near sundown. Their nerves'll be all frazzled and they won't be able to hit the broadside of a henhouse. Yer pappy used to say, when their nerves are shot all to hell, they can't shoot *you* to hell. We're goin' in all right, but not until I'm ready."

"What about Slug?" Little Bo asked. "They see us

a-comin', they'll kill him fer sure."

"Shit, boy, he's as good as dead even if he ain't already. Serves the stupid peckerwood right fer gettin' caught." Ma walked to the table and peered out the cabin window. The Mallorys had been unceremoniously dumped into the well. Most of the boys were scattered around the ranch, trying to catch a few winks.

"This ain't like you, Ma," Hank said. "Time was, you'd be the one rushin' in and me'n the boys be tryin' to hold you back. Seems to me like maybe yer goin' a little soft."

Ma barely blinked, turned, and pulled out a pistol, which she fired dead center into Hank's right kneecap. Blood and bone fragments flew as Hank crashed to the floor and started bellowing in pain. Preacher started cackling hysterically.

"Jesus, Ma," Little Bo cried. "What'd you do that fer?"

Ma looked down at her son as he howled and clutched his shattered knee. Her voice dripping with venom, Ma said, "Now every time you take a step, you'll remember how soft I am."

She turned to Little Bo and said, "You think I'm soft, boy?"

"No, Ma," Little Bo said, his face whiter than snow. "Shit no."

Ma shoved her pistol back into her petticoat. She gave the room a toothless grin. "I got me a hankerin' for a man. The thought of some hard killin' ahead always makes me frisky."

Her eyes roamed around the room. Her sons stared down at the floor, not daring to meet her gaze.

She settled on Mortimer, her third oldest and the

largest of her brood. "I got me an itch, Mortimer," she said, "and you got to scratch it for me."

While the others sighed in relief, Mortimer, with his Adam's apple bobbing nervously, gasped, "B-but Ma, I got to tend to the horses—"

Ma fired a shot into the ceiling and screeched, "Shut your pie hole, boy. It's yer turn!"

"Can't we draw straws like last time?" Mortimer sputtered. "You said—"

Ma ignored him. "The rest of you vermin, git the hell out so's to give me an' my boy some privacy. And haul his sorry butt out of here, too," Ma said, motioning to Hank, who was howling in agony.

Wordlessly, Bo and Little Bo hoisted their brother to his foot—his shot leg was dangling uselessly—and dragged him out the door.

"I'll get her fer this," Hank muttered to Little Bo.

"Count yer blessin's," Little Bo muttered back, "least you ain't in Mortimer's shoes now."

"Patch him up," Ma barked. To Hank, she said, "You be ready to ride, son, or I'll leave you for buzzards.

"Move!" she snapped, kicking Preacher, the last one out, squarely in the butt. She slammed the door and turned to her remaining son. She grinned toothlessly.

Mortimer looked like he wanted to cry.

"I've heard tell of this Ma Fisher," Slocum said. He was sitting alone at a table in the saloon. The ranchers, in a show of respect, sat in a semicircle around him.

"She's got us sweating, just what she wants,"

Slocum went on. "Could come in a minute, in an hour, a day and a half, who the hell knows? Trick is to be ready and alert, like when a pack of coyotes come down on your chicken coop."

"You got a plan, Slocum?" Jonah Wilbershot said as he studied his fingernails.

"Been thinkin' on it," he said.

Slocum had dispatched Geezer to a spot called Cutler's Ridge a few miles out of town, where the old duffer could spot the Fishers two miles off— *if* they decided to ride straight into town. There was always the chance the Fishers would split up and attack Roseville from four directions. And who would know best Ma Fisher's favorite plan of attack, Slocum told them, but one of Ma's own sons?

"When did we feed Slug Fisher last?" Slocum asked.

Rose answered, "Twelve hours, maybe more. We've had other things to worry about."

"Good," Slocum said. "I think I'll pay him a visit."

"I'm hongry," Slug snapped as Slocum came through the door.

"Shut your trap," Slocum said, and walked to the cell. He reached through the bars and grabbed a fistful of Slug's shirt and yanked him forward. Slug's head clunked soundly against the iron bars.

"How old are you, boy?" Slocum asked.

"I was ten 'bout nine years ago," Slug answered. "How old is that?"

"Old enough," Slocum said, his nose an inch away from Slug's. "And how long you been riding with your ma?"

"Long's I-I remember," Slug stammered, Slocum's cold, deadly stare was making him nervous—and cooperative.

"And how many towns like this have you and your ma rode into?"

"A bunch," Slug said.

Slocum released him and pulled the key to the cell from his pocket. He unlocked the cell, walked in, and slammed the door shut. Slug stepped back out of fear, his eyes were wide as Slocum thrust his hand out and shoved Slug backwards. Slug crashed down onto the cot. Slocum pulled out his Colt, jammed the barrel into Slug's mouth, and cocked the trigger.

"Just one more question," Slocum said, "and I'd appreciate an honest answer. Do we have a deal?"

Slug nodded vigorously.

Slocum asked "How's your ma going to ride in?"

He pulled the gun out of Slug's mouth. Slug swallowed hard, his eyes wide.

"She'll be ridin' in on a horse," Slug said in all seriousness.

"That answer don't satisfy me, Slug," Slocum said patiently, and aimed the Colt at Slug's face. "How's she usually ride into a town like this? She comin' straight on in, or from all sides?"

"Ma don't believe in bein' fancy," Slug said. "She'll ride in snortin' like a bull."

"Much better," Slocum said. "When'll she make her move?"

"Cain't say fer certain," Slug said, "but when she does, you'll sure as hell know." Slug's beady eyes glinted. "You gonna kill me?"

"You feel like dyin'?"

"Not right now," Slug said.

"That means you feel like stayin' alive," Slocum confirmed.

"I reckon it does," Slug admitted, slightly confused.

"Fine," Slocum said, holstering his Colt and unlocking the cell door, his back to Slug. Slug leaped up at Slocum and got an elbow in the jaw for his trouble. Slug's head snapped back like a cap on a bottle of sarsaparilla. He tumbled flat onto his skinny ass.

Slocum stepped out of the jail cell and shut the door, giving the key a twist.

"Play your cards right, Slug," Slocum said, "and maybe you'll live through the next few hours."

Slug rubbed his jaw, shaking his head to clear what little was in it. "I'm still hongry," he moaned.

"Swallow some more pride," Slocum said. "It's good for you."

"We'll need some rope, two sections of twenty feet each," Slocum said as he and Rose rummaged through the abandoned mercantile after Slocum had kicked the door open. "And nails, and as much lard and soap as this store holds."

"Lard? Soap?" Rose asked. "Now ain't the time to think of a bath—"

"And grab every box of bullets you can lay your hands on," Slocum said.

"In the back are two barrels," Rose told him, grabbing as much rope as she could. "In one is molasses, in the other you'll find nails. Help yourself."

"We'll need to boil the soap and lard, keep it hot until the Fishers ride in for sure," Slocum said. "Fire up every potbelly in town." Slocum made his way to the back of the mercantile and saw a mattress wrapped in torn brown paper leaning against the wall of the stockroom. He whipped out a pocketknife and started slashing it, a clump of feathers spat out in his face.

"Goose down," Slocum said. "Perfect."

"Anytime you want to tell me what your plan is, John," Rose said, "feel free."

"When I get it all figured, I will," Slocum said. "Meantime, I'll need the feathers from this mattress."

"Don't think I won't deduct the cost of this mysterious plan of yours from your salary," Rose commented dryly.

"And don't think I didn't expect you not to," he said.

Geezer was there to help out. Once he had everything he needed, Slocum told Geezer to tie one end of the ropes around a pillar in front of the hotel and unravel the rest across Main Street, then leave the other end at the door of the mercantile.

"Cover the rope with street dust so it can't be seen," Slocum instructed him.

Geezer did just that. At around the same time, Owen Grey rode into town and dismounted as Slocum was escorting Slug Fisher across the street to the church. Slug had his hands tied tightly behind his back and looked grim.

"Got that hundred head of cattle right outside town, just like you told me, Slocum," Grey said, dismounting and wiping his sweaty face with a bandanna. "What now?"

"Go back to 'em," Slocum said, "and whenever

Geezer or me gives you a signal, herd 'em right down Main Street."

"What kind of signal?" Grey wanted to know.

"When you start hearing a lot of people shooting and screaming, move 'em on in," Slocum said. "How's that?"

"Could work," Grey answered, and mounted up. He reined his bay back toward the outskirts of town. "When you think the Fishers'll make their move?" he asked.

Slocum scratched his chin. "Damned if I know," he answered. "I suspect Ma will try to wear us out, maybe catch us with our britches down. Middle of night, I'd say, maybe sooner, 'round midnight." He sighed tiredly. "We best be as ready as ready can be. Drink lots of coffee and keep your chambers filled."

"I ain't much of a shot, Slocum," Grey admitted. "Slow as molasses, to be honest."

"Don't fret none," Slocum told him. "Fast is fine, but accuracy is final."

"My ma's gonna blow yer butt off," Slug ranted at a nervous Owen Grey. "You just wait! She's a-gonna ram the barrel of her gun up your poop chute an'—"

Slocum grabbed a thick clump of Slug's unruly hair and jerked the outlaw's head back. Slug yelped in pain.

"That'll be enough, buffalo brain," Slocum said, shoving Slug's noggin forward. He gave Slug a healthy knock on the skull for good measure.

Grey spurred his bay and trotted off. Slocum escorted Slug to the church, opened the door, and pushed him inside. Slug flew straight into the last row of pews and tumbled over it, falling ass backwards.

He looked up at Slocum with a hurt look on his beady-eyed mug. "What fer'd ya do that?"

Slocum walked over and grabbed Slug by the collar, jerking him to his feet. "Get used to it," Slocum said, and shoved Slug toward the back of the church. As they passed the altar, he added, "You got any prayers you feel like sayin', you best say 'em now."

"I don't fear no false gods, like Ma says," Slug responded.

"You may want to think about startin'," Slocum said, pushing Slug through another door at the back of the church and into a dark storeroom. There was a ladder that led up to the steeple, where a huge bell—paid for by Rose herself, her gift to the good people of Roseville—had recently been added.

"Climb," Slocum ordered, untying Slug's hands.

"What fer?" Slug asked, rubbing his wrists.

"Shut up and do it." Slocum slammed Slug into the rickety wooden ladder. "And don't try anything dumb or I'll kill you here and now." Slug dutifully started climbing, with Slocum right behind him. Pissing Slocum off, Slug knew, tended to hurt.

Slug pushed open the trapdoor to the steeple and climbed up. There was a length of rope waiting in a corner, and one end was tied into a noose.

Slocum scrambled through the trapdoor and pointed to the noose. "Try it on for size, Slug," he said.

Slug looked sour but did as he was told. Slocum tied Slug's hands behind his back again, then tightened the noose so it fit nice and snug.

"What you gonna do, Slocum?" Slug asked, his

voice quavering, near cracking.

"It's a surprise," Slocum said with a grin. "You'll like it."

"Will I?" Slug asked, fearing the worst.

Slocum shrugged. "Probably not."

By five, every piece of Slocum's plan was falling into place. Jonah Wilbershot was perched on the roof of the bank with an old but reliable Sharps at his side. A burlap bag filled with goose feathers sat nearby. *Damn, if that Slocum wasn't some kind of genius*, Jonah thought.

Next door, two of Charlie Russell's hands, Cal Fletcher and Jake Keen, crouched on the roof of Mr. Drake's bakery; they were heavily armed. Two burlap sacks filled with goose feathers sat ready and waiting. They'd taken the liberty of borrowing the few day-old pies and cakes old man Drake had left behind in the bakery before grabbing his daughter, little Debbie, and fleeing town. Now, they sat and devoured the delectable treats.

"This is better'n Christmas," Cal said to Jake.

Jake sucked down half a blueberry pie; his face was blue and sticky. "Sure is," he said with a resounding belch.

Across the street, Charlie Russell nibbled on a coffee cake also commandeered from Drake's Bakery. He was perched low on the roof of the cafe. As with the others, a bag of goose feathers was kept handy. Downstairs, Reverend Horton continued to stir four huge pots of lye soap and lard boiling on the stove. He hummed "Bringing in the Sheaves."

Further down the street, on the roof of the mercantile, Abel Gormly finished a bag of sugar cookies—also courtesy of Mr. Drake—and patted his substantial belly. Gormly had heard of some wild schemes before, but none matched the sheer ingenuity of Slocum's. If things worked out right, the Fisher gang would soon be but a bad memory.

"Goose feathers," Gormly grunted to himself. "Who'd've thunked it?"

Owen Grey was atop the roof of the hotel, waiting anxiously for the fur to start flying, not to mention the feathers. Every now and then he would throw a wave to one of the others on the rooftops. They were all scared, Grey knew, but somehow it hadn't affected their appetites.

Downstairs in the hotel lobby, Rose sat behind the desk and sighed, boredom and tension both wearing her down. Slocum paced back and forth, puffing a smoke and wracking his brain for any neglected last minute details. The few hotel guests—a couple of Kansas City drummers and an elderly widow on her way to Abilene—had long since cleared out at Rose's suggestion. It was just the two of them, waiting for all hell to break loose.

Rose toyed with the bell on the front desk, tapping it lightly and making small *dings* ring out. She was bored, despite the fact that there was every chance her town might be reduced to cinders before the day was over.

Slocum continued pacing, tension oozing from every pore. "Wish the bastards would show their miserable asses so we could get this over with."

"Sit down and relax, John," Rose said. "You've done everything possible and then some. Our fate is in the hands of the Almighty now."

"I don't know anybody in this damned town,"

Slocum snapped. "Don't know if they're reliable. Half of 'em can't piss in a straight line, much less shoot—"

"Now, John," Rose said, coming from behind the desk and easing Slocum gently into a finely upholstered chair. "You just take a load off and breathe easy."

Slocum sat. Rose stood behind him and gently rubbed his chest, then ran her fingers through his hair.

"We're going to beat them, John," Rose said soothingly. "Don't you worry your cute little head."

"What makes you so sure?" he asked as Rose's left hand dropped down to his crotch. She unzipped his fly and darted her hand inside, probing for the riches. She found them, and curled her delicate fingers around his fleshy saddle horn, which immediately rose to the occasion.

"Because we have you on our side, that's what," she said, giving him a gentle squeeze.

Slocum pulled her face down and kissed her hard on the lips. "You're one special lady, you know that?"

"Yes," she said, "but I never get tired of hearing it." She kissed him back, even harder, then whispered, "Want to make some love?"

Slocum looked up at Rose and gazed deeply into her blazing blue eyes. "What's in it for me?" he asked.

"That depends," Rose cooed. "You only get out what you put in."

Slocum rose from the chair and pulled her close. His hands slid down to her tight buttocks, clenching them. He backed Rose up against the wall and pressed her against it, kissing her neck and throat hungrily. She wrapped her legs around his waist and her arms around his neck. He rubbed his crotch against her and they kissed passionately, despite the sense of urgency and the gray shadow of death barely outside their door.

Slocum ripped open her blouse and started pawing at her plump, full breasts, wanting only to plant his lips on her ripe nipples and suckle them deeply.

"Easy, cowboy," Rose said softly in his ear.

"Easy hell," Slocum grunted back. "This could be our last chance." He kissed her hard on the mouth. "That honeymoon suite still available?"

Rose squirmed out of his grasp and walked over to the desk, fussing with her hair. She opened the reservation book and flipped through the thick pages.

She looked up at Slocum, her pretty face a sweaty mask of desire.

"I believe it is," she said.

Slocum started to go to her, ready to take her on the staircase if necessary. Rose picked up the quill pen and held it out to him. "You have to sign in first, sir." She spun the register book to face him.

Slocum grabbed the pen and jotted down, "*Eat me.*" He spun the book back around.

"That'll be one dollar in advance," she said.

"That's kind of stiff," Slocum protested.

"From the looks of it, so are you," she said. Slocum self-consciously took off his Stetson and covered the bulge in his groin with it.

"Oh, don't be so modest, Slocum," Rose said, pushing the hat away. "It's men like you that tamed the West," she said, taking his hand and guiding him up the stairs. "And to think—we women never even said thank you."

She steered him into one of the empty rooms, then shut the door with the back of her foot. She eased Slocum down onto the bed so that he was flat on his back. She grabbed his hat and flung it across the room, then straddled him on the bed and went to work unbuckling his gun belt. That done, she really got down to business, yanking his pants down around his ankles and reaching inside his long underwear.

"Unfortunately, we have no time for the preliminaries," she whispered softly, and took his rock-hard shaft between her lips, sliding it halfway into her mouth.

"Pity," Slocum said, and groaned in ecstasy as Rose caressed the underside of his manhood with her velvety tongue, her head nodding up and down vigorously, as if in joyous agreement.

Slocum gripped the brass bars of the bed frame as Rose lovingly cupped his balls in her hand and gave them a playful squeeze. An hour or two of this, he thought, might be nice.

She gripped the base of his cock with one hand and slid her other hand under his shirt, rubbing his chest. Slocum swallowed hard and started breathing faster as she skillfully brought him closer to the brink. She slid his saliva-slickened shaft in and out between her lips. Slocum was putty in her hands, albeit hard putty.

"Oh, Rose," Slocum gasped, biting a finger for no good reason he could think of, unless it was to keep him from bouncing off the ceiling. Every sweet thrust of Rose's mouth on his member brought him dangerously close to exploding. She gurgled happily, swallowing him up to the base. Slocum guided her now, running his fingers through her silky hair.

He was moments from erupting when Rose slid her mouth off his swollen cock and, still straddling him, lifted her dress, and poised directly over him. She was wearing absolutely nothing underneath, Slocum saw with both amazement and delight.

"You never know where the day may take you," Rose commented, reading his mind perfectly. She grabbed his manhood and sat on it, sliding it deep inside her. She rocked back and forth, her legs splayed out on either side of his thighs. Slocum reached up and grabbed her breasts, giving himself to her completely.

It was maybe a minute later, as his balls became tender and he felt an incredibly pleasant sensation in his groin, that shots rang out. Slocum was mere seconds from coming when Rose abruptly stopped bouncing. He was half in and half out of her at the time.

"Damn!" Slocum cried.

Rose was about to climb off of him, but Slocum grabbed her hips frantically and slammed her back down.

"What are you doing?" Rose asked indignantly. "The Fishers—"

"No," Slocum gasped, knowing the tortuous pain in his crotch that awaited him if he and Rose didn't finish consummating this all-too-brief interlude. "It's j-just Geezer," he stammered. "Please, finish me off. Otherwise—"

"Are you crazy?" she responded, and hopped off him. She ran to the window, jerking the stiff curtains aside.

Slocum, forgetting that his pants were bunched up around his ankles, scrambled off the bed. He got maybe six inches before his ankles twisted and he crashed flat on his face most ungracefully. The pleasurable stirring in his balls was rapidly turning painful. Blue balls, he'd heard it called once—when a man didn't complete what nature intended him to.

"This shit's gettin' on my nerves," he mumbled.

Outside, just as Slocum had predicted, Geezer came galloping down Main Street, crying, "The Fishers are headin' in! Two miles from town. Be breathin' down our necks right soon!"

Norval Jones's sons, Egbert and Donald, were both asleep in chairs on opposite sides of Main Street. Egbert slumbered in front of the mercantile, while Donald dozed peacefully in front of the bank. It took two more shots from Geezer before they awakened. Not quite on cue, they both grabbed their ends of the rope and pulled, making it spring up a good six inches—and just in time for Geezer's mare to trip up and stumble over it.

"Son of a whore," Geezer yelped, and went tumbling forward in the saddle as the horse collapsed to its knees. He hit the street and rolled a few times, coming to rest in a mud puddle.

He sat up with mud dripping down his face, and cackled, "You dumb peckerwood jackasses!" Egbert and Donald ran to him and each grabbed an elbow, bringing Geezer unsteadily to his feet. Geezer pushed them away and shook the wet mud off his person, splattering the brothers with it.

"Didn't you see it was me?" Geezer chastised, wiping mud from his beard and flinging it in their fat faces.

"It was Egbert," Donald said. "He fell asleep!"

"Weren't such," Egbert said. "I wuz just pretendin', to fool the Fishers. If you—"

"Both of you shut your mouths," Slocum barked from the third-floor hotel window, pulling up his pants. His balls were already throbbing painfully from the rude interruption. "Let's move!"

Slocum wrapped his gun belt around his waist and buckled it tight. Rose was already out the door and halfway downstairs. In a locked broom closet in the kitchen were more guns than Slocum had ever seen: Winchesters, Colts, and Smith & Wessons. She was flinging the door open as Slocum came down the stairs. He saw her private arsenal and whistled loudly.

"Woman, you been holdin' back," he said, visibly impressed.

"This is Texas," she said, and tossed him a rifle, "a lady can't be too careful."

"Reckon not," Slocum observed. He cracked it open—both barrels were loaded and ready to pump, which was more than he was capable of at that moment. Frustrating pain from his agonized balls came in waves now, and it made him madder than a hornet in heat. The Fishers were wholly responsible for all of his suffering—and they were going to pay for it.

Slocum walked outside. Each step was a new adventure in pain, as if two inflamed billiard balls were knocking around inside his scrotum. All of a sudden, walking upright hurt. Slocum shook off the pain below the belt and watched the scene unfold. Geezer was trying to separate Egbert and Donald Jones from landing blows on each other.

"Save it for them Fishers," Geezer advised. "You're gonna need it."

"Are they at least drunk?" Slocum asked. "Give us an edge if they was."

"Cold sober," Geezer said, "and ridin' harder than their looks."

"Damn," Slocum cursed, and went inside to raid Rose's arsenal again. He grabbed another rifle—a Winchester .44. To this, he added a Colt Peacemaker, which he shoved under his belt, and a Remington New Model Army .44, which he shoved into his left boot. Also on the shelf was a nasty looking item, a barrelless gun that evidently shot directly out of the chamber. Slocum examined it. "Where'd you get this thing?"

"From Klein's Mail Order Weapon Emporium, Brooklyn, New York," she said. "It's called a knuckle-duster. Doubles as a bludgeon." Rose took it from him and squeezed off a shot from the squatty little gun. It took out an impressive chunk of the front desk. She fired another, and the check-in bell exploded.

"Never did like that thing," Rose said, and handed it back to Slocum. She went to the closet and started grabbing a few weapons for herself.

Slocum asked, "What are you doing?"

"Defending myself, what the hell does it look like?" Slocum knew that beneath her bravado, she was scared shitless.

"Rose," Slocum said, "you don't know how to shoot that well, remember? I'd be much happier if you were out of the line of fire. I was thinking along the lines of locking yourself in a fruit cellar somewhere 'til this tornado blows out of town."

"Oh you would?" she asked.

"That's what I was thinking, yes," he answered.

"Let's not argue about this, John, darling." She patted his cheek and reached for a reliable Remington ten-gauge shotgun. Slocum thought crazily the rifle looked dainty cradled in her arms.

"You're right," Slocum said. "Let's not argue." He grabbed her around the waist and roughly hoisted her over his shoulder. She flailed her arms and kicked wildly, but to no avail. Slocum held her firmly and made his way to the dank, dingy basement of the restaurant. The sweet-sour aroma of overripe fruit and ghosts of old sauerkraut filled their nostrils as he threw open the door and descended down the stairs.

"You dirty bastard!" she yelled, kicking and pounding his back with her tiny fists. "You dirty, disgusting, lice-ridden son of a bitch! You no-good prairie-tramp, sheep-screwing, cactus-hugging—"

"You best stop now, Rose, 'fore you call me something that really offends me." He reached the bottom of the steps and deposited Rose down firmly in a barrel of dill pickles. She was covered up to her middle with green brine.

"This is *my* town, Slocum," she bellowed as he went up the stairs. "This is *my* fight. How much am I paying you?" She pointed an accusatory finger at him.

"What difference does that make?" he asked.

"Whatever it is, I'll double it," she said.

"Agreed," Slocum said, and went up more stairs.

"Fine," Rose snapped. "Now you're fired." She hopped out of the barrel, brine piddling in a puddle at her feet. She started coming up the stairs. Slocum held his palm out, motioning for her to stop. "You take one step, you go back in the barrel headfirst."

She looked hard at him; her eyes were cold. She went up two steps and stopped.

"Make that four steps," Slocum said.

Rose made it six. Slocum was on her like a shot, and back over his shoulder she went. Making good on his word, this time he plopped her down headfirst into the pickle barrel. Bubbles quickly rose to the surface as Rose kicked her legs frantically, trying to extract herself. By the time she had, Slocum was at the top of the stairs and pushing the thick wooden door open. Rose, ever the vigilant innkeeper had wisely put a strong lock on the fruit cellar door. Her hair was dripping with brine and a huge pickle was lodged in her mouth. She spat it out and snapped, "You aren't locking me in here."

"Yes I am," Slocum said, and went through the doorway. He slammed the door shut and locked it with a key hanging conveniently on a nail on the side of a cabinet.

"You six-gun pond scum," he heard her yell from below.

"Just sit tight, Rosie," Slocum called back to her. "You'll be safe down there."

"Until one of the Fishers sees fit to burn this place to the ground!" she yelled, her voice muffled behind the thick wooden door.

"We're gonna see that don't happen," Slocum said, and strode out into the street.

A gentle breeze blew little eddies of dust up and down Main Street. Otherwise, the town was seemingly deserted. Slocum knew better. The ranchers were hidden in various spots all over town, including the rooftops. Egbert and Donald Jones, Slocum could see, were alert and manning the rope. He made his way down the street to the church.

Inside, some of the ranch hands were sitting in the last two rows of pews. Earl Burns, Eric Judd, and Sam Snyder worked for Mike Bannon at the Bar B. They'd bravely offered their services to help defend the town—though Rose's offer for fifty dollars per dead Fisher was an added inducement. They were clad in full battle gear—from the wardrobes of half the women in Roscville. All three were wearing Sunday-best dresses and their dirt-streaked, unshaven faces peered out from under sky blue bonnets. Even more incongruous was their rendering of "Just a Closer Walk With Thee" in high-pitched voices with Bibles in their calloused hands. Up on the pulpit, Reverend Horton led his small, well-armed congregation in the off-key singing. Leaning against the wall was an upright, open casket. Inside, Geezer lay with his arms crossed, making a very convincing stiff.

All, it appeared, was in readiness.

Slocum went up to the steeple where Slug Fisher was tied and waiting.

Ma sent in Little Bo and two others first. Little Bo was flanked by Nails Henry, who was a lot worse for the wear having been dragged by a horse a few days earlier, and a vicious, swarthy half-breed from the Oklahoma Territory known simply as Red. The product of a drunken trail bum father and a Cherokee mother, Red was especially handy with a knife; he could slice the pubic hairs off a mouse at twenty-five yards. He joined up with the Fishers back in north Texas a few weeks earlier; he was on the run from a bloody murder back in Tulsa. Red had buried a knife deep into the belly of a marshal's deputy who'd tried to arrest him for yet another murder—of a cheap, consumptive whore in a fifty-cent crib. Red had delighted in the sensation of the deputy's life filtering through his hand and up his arm while his knife twisted in the surprised lawman's guts. After the fire of life flickered out of the deputy's eyes, the look of shock never left them. Even now, as they rode into an uncertain situation with death hanging around every bend, Red smiled at the memory.

On the outskirts of town, Little Bo could see that the place was deserted. No doubt about it, he knew. They were expected.

Little Bo signaled for them to stop, which they did.

"Too quiet for me," he murmured.

Spurs hit flanks. Little Bo turned and headed back to Ma and the others, who were waiting half a mile out of town. Nails Henry and Red followed behind.

Slocum watched with some displeasure from the church steeple. He'd hoped they could at least pick off these three, which would lessen the odds. Then again, maybe Little Bo would tell Ma that the town had been cleared out and was theirs for the taking. They'd come in hard, hell for leather, putting holes in anything that didn't have them. The Fishers would be less cautious, thinking the town was deserted—and that much easier to pick off.

Again, Slocum was disappointed.

The Fishers came, but came in slowly, an hour later. Slocum hoped Egbert and Donald were smart enough not to try the rope trick on them at their slow pace. Slocum ducked down the steeple.

• • •

"I got a bad feelin' about this," Ma Fisher said.

"Me too," Bo commented.

The breeze shifted, coming out of the north, and suddenly they could hear the off-key singing from the church.

"Praise the Lord," Preacher chirped. "They're worshippin'."

"Go check it out," she said to the wiry Jesus jumper.

Preacher happily dismounted and ambled over to the church, waving his Bible. He joined in on the singing.

He flung the church door open and was greeted by the sight of a funeral. The last thing he saw was Geezer laid out in the coffin and Reverend leading the singing. Barely a second after Preacher stepped inside, the three ranch hands turned and let loose a barrage that peppered the Preacher with lead. He flew backwards out onto the street, bullet holes, almost a dozen in all, riddling his worthless carcass. Half his face was now decorating the walls of the church. The Bible was still clutched in his fist.

With this, the ranchers on the rooftops opened fire, but unfortunately, the Fishers were far enough down the street so that the shots missed by yards.

"Shit," Slocum said. This wasn't working out at all.

The gang's first reaction was to turn tail and run, but Ma Fisher, in the face of the gunfire, didn't even flinch. As the others started spurring their horses to flee, Ma barked out, "Where the hell do you think y'all are going? We came to get my boy, an' we ain't leavin' 'til we do."

With an earsplitting shriek she spurred her horse and galloped off down the middle of Main Street, firing at rooftops. The rest of the gang followed her, and the gunplay started in earnest.

Hank Fisher was the first to go down, with a bullet in his throat from Charlie Russell's rifle. Ma's larcenous litter was now reduced by one. Ma didn't grieve though; she had no time for that nonsense.

"Ma's gone plum loco," Little Bo cried out.

"Tell me somethin' I don't know," Bo said.

12

Even without any protective cover, Ma and her boys still managed to do some heavy damage.

Firing from the top of the bakery, Jake Kern took a chunk of lead from Ma's gun. The bullet blew off half his jaw and went straight up into his brain. He was dead before he tumbled off the roof and plummeted to the street.

Nails Henry, not nearly as foolhardy as the rest of the Fishers, ducked behind a horse trough, directly underneath the bank. Seeing him from above, Jonah Wilbershot tipped a bucket full of hot, bubbling lard and soap and poured it down. Nails looked up just in time to see the steaming ooze and barely had time to blink when the scorching liquid splattered in his face, cooking his eyeballs like dumplings. This was followed by a bucketful of feathers from the mattress.

Nails let out a cry of agony and staggered right into the middle of Main Street. Slocum ended Henry's torment with a bullet in the brain. Nails tumbled facedown into the dust.

"They just hammered Nails," Little Bo said as lead whizzed by his head.

The ranchers were firing wildly, hitting horses, the street, and everything but the intended targets. Earl Burns and Eric Judd, shooting from the doorway of the church, were mad as hell that their boss, Mike Bannon, was dead. Burns fired at Bo Fisher, hitting his horse in the side and in one of its hind legs. The dun went down and Bo went sprawling. He barely touched dirt before he was up and shooting, taking Earl Burns twice in the gut. Meanwhile, Ma brought down Abel Gormly with a couple in the belly.

"This is bad," Slocum muttered to himself, surveying the damage. He turned to Slug and grabbed him roughly by the shoulder, jerking him to his feet. "You're on, boy," he said. Slocum had taken the added precaution of tightening the noose extra snugly around Slug's neck. In no position to refuse, especially with Slocum's gun at his temple, Slug stepped out onto the narrow ledge of the steeple. Slocum turned and gave the church bell rope a hefty yank.

The gong was deafening, but it had the desired effect. The shooting stopped, miraculously, just long enough for Slocum to stick the barrel of his gun in Slug's back. Slug swayed to and fro, threatening to fall. Slocum grabbed him by the belt and hollered, "One more shot and your boy is dead!"

Ma and her boys looked up to see their brother Slug tottering above them on the wall of the steeple.

Ma, crouching behind a dead horse, stood up and looked at her baby with his hands bound behind his back and a noose around his neck.

"I'll give you one minute to clear out, or Slug'll dance on air!" Slocum called down.

"Do what he says, Ma," Slug cried. "Fer Gawd's sake!"

"I'm deeply disappointed in you, son," Ma called back, and squeezed off a bullet that slammed into Slug's forehead. He fell backwards into Slocum and they sprawled to the steeple floor.

"So much for that idea," Slocum said, pushing Slug's lifeless body away.

The shooting began again. Slocum watched in amazement as Ma, not exactly light on her feet, skillfully zigzagged across the street and disappeared as if by magic. The ranchers were busy trying to blast the rest of the Fishers. Jonah Wilbershot caught Bo Fisher in the back of the head. As he flopped dead into the mud, Ma, behind a wooden pillar, fired twice and took off a chuck of Wilbershot's shoulder. Old Jonah fell backwards, his Sharps rifle flying from his hands. It landed squarely on Mortimer Fisher's thick noggin down below. Mortimer staggered a few times and sank down to his ass, semiconscious.

At that instant, a thundering roar came from the west end of Main Street. One hundred head of spooked cattle came cascading into town in a brown wave that engulfed Main Street. The half-breed Red dashed to his horses and lit out.

Slocum caught him between the shoulder blades with two well-placed shots. Mortimer, sitting dazed in the street, didn't hear the stampeding cattle, who filled the wooden walkways and trampled everything in their path.

Mortimer Fisher rose unsteadily to his feet. His head was beginning to clear when he saw the herd of beef barely yards from where he stood. Before he could even turn to run, he was knocked down by one indignant cow. Before he could draw a breath, the stampeding herd was on him; a million hooves stomping his face and insides into a mass of red jelly.

Slocum was already on his way down the ladder into the chapel as the herd trampled everything in their path. The walls of the church seemed to vibrate as the cattle stormed past down the middle of Roseville's Main Street. The Reverend Horton was crouching behind the altar like a scared rabbit. Geezer and the ranch hands were reloading frantically. Ma and Little Bo had pulled a vanishing act sometime during the stampede. They were nowhere to be found.

"Did 'em some damage," Geezer said to Slocum, jamming a cartridge into the chamber of his rifle. "Just Ma and one of her boys left, and if we don't bring her down right quick more folks is gonna die."

"Anybody see where they went?" Slocum yelled out. The last of the cattle were plodding through town as they stepped outside. Once the rumbling stopped, Roseville was eerily quiet. A few head still lingered in the street as the dust settled, a little bewildered, sniffing the dead bodies before moving on.

Across the street, from a rooftop, Charlie Russell called back, "Disappeared somewhere near the hotel, I think."

"You sure?" Slocum shouted.

Before Russell could answer, two shots sliced through the silence. They came from inside the hotel.

● ● ●

Rose was rummaging through the cellar for anything that might smash through a wooden door. Above her, the entire hotel was shaking as the cattle *shlepped* through town. Dirt and dust sprinkled down from between the floorboards above her, choking her.

She found an ax next to a tinderbox, then dashed up the steps as the rumbling continued. She'd read newspaper accounts of earthquakes in Peru, Mexico, and even in San Francisco and imagined they might have been like this.

She spat into her palms and started swinging at the door. Hunks of wood flew into her face and hair. Like a woman possessed, she hacked away at the lock and the door like a woodsman in the forests of Bavaria. She didn't hear the footsteps above her.

"It's just you and me now, Ma," Little Bo whispered to his mother.

They were skulking through the hotel dining room, ready to blast anything that moved, looking for a way out the back. Ma was sure they could make good an escape if they could get to the horses they'd left outside.

She was already figuring out how to recruit a new gang of rogues once they made it to Mexico. She shed no tears for her fallen sons. If they were stupid enough to get themselves killed, she reasoned, then they deserved to die.

Running in the cattle, Ma mused, was a damn good idea. She wished she could think up smart shit like that. Somehow, Ma Fisher was convinced her friend Slocum had come up with it. More men like him in her gang, she decided, could be a good thing. Quantrill would have approved. All she'd had were a bunch of idiot sons, each one dumber than the low-down bastards who'd helped conceive them, slimy rats she'd loved for the time it took for them to shoot their seed between her beefy thighs.

Ma's head jerked instinctively toward the kitchen as the sounds of someone pounding away with an ax echoed through the dining room. Little Bo spun on his heels, six-shooter already pointing in the direction of the kitchen.

Rose chopped away until she could see the kitchen through a hole in the door six inches above the doorknob. She reached through the hole, clutching the ax in her other hand, and unlocked the damn door. The fat was sizzling on the fire and she was missing all the heat. She wanted to be a part of the fight, and that bastard Slocum hadn't let her.

Adrenaline coursing through her veins, she grabbed the doorknob, gave it a twist, and opened the door from the outside. The harsh sunlight coming through the kitchen window temporarily blinded her, just long enough for Ma and Little Bo to dash into the kitchen. They were greeted with the sight of a madwoman blinking rapidly and clutching an ax.

Rose focused her eyes and saw Ma Fisher in the flesh, a formidable figure, aiming a .45 directly at her, as was some dirty-faced man standing next to her. Rose caught a glimpse of Ma grimacing, showing a couple of rotted teeth, and felt herself being knocked backwards through the open cellar door as Ma's gun exploded. A huge roar filled the kitchen, and then the man next to Ma Fisher fired three times. Pain seared through Rose's chest and belly as she smashed against the wall and spun around, then she went bouncing down the steps to the cellar floor. She lay sprawled on her side with her ribs bruised and blood oozing from the holes in her body.

"Son of a bitch," Rose gasped, and the warm comfort of darkness engulfed her.

Ma and Little Bo were already out the side door and running into the alley between the hotel and the blacksmith's as the last of the cattle stampeded down Main Street. There were only a few houses behind Main Street and then the wide open expanse of west Texas beyond that. A couple of the gang's horses were grazing in a vegetable garden in the front of one of the houses.

"Looks like Hank's mare, Mortimer's, too," Little Bo said.

"They got no more use for 'em," Ma croaked, "but we do."

"We gonna make a run for it, Ma?" Little Bo asked.

"No," she said, and slapped him hard across his ugly face. "I thought we'd stay around for the church supper." She ran to the horses. Little Bo dutifully followed. They saddled up and were gone, heading south.

"Rose!" Slocum called out as he and Geezer made their way through the hotel and into the kitchen. Slocum first saw the open cellar door, then the puddle of blood on the floor.

"Don't look good," Geezer said.

Slocum peered through the door. Rose was lying on her side, one leg splayed over the bottom step. Her torso was soaked with blood.

He took the stairs two at a time and knelt beside her, grabbing her hand. It was still warm. He put his ear to her chest and heard a faint heartbeat. Her pulse was weak. She was alive—barely.

Her eyes fluttered open. Blood oozed from the corner of her mouth and ran down her cheek.

"I'm here," Slocum said.

"You're late," she said.

"Was it Ma Fisher?" Slocum asked.

Rose rasped, "You think I did this to myself?"

Even close to death, Rose was good for a cynical remark. He was barely aware of Geezer coming downstairs and kneeling beside him.

"Where's Doc Phipps?" Slocum asked.

"On his way, soon's I fetch him," Geezer said. "Keep her warm and don't try to move her 'til I get back."

"I ain't stupid," Slocum snapped. "Get moving."

Geezer got moving.

He clutched Rose's hand and gave it a gentle squeeze.

"Don't worry, baby," Slocum whispered. "Help's on its way."

"I don't feel so good," she said, coughing. Blood bubbled to her lips. "You may be sleeping alone tonight."

"Shut up," Slocum said. "Doc Phipps'll be here in a minute."

"Better call Reverend Horton instead," she said. "I'm not a Christian, but a rabbi is hard to find around here."

She coughed again, fading before his eyes. Damn if he didn't feel a tear creep from the corner of his eye. He clenched his eyes shut to force the tear back, but it was there to stay.

"Do me a favor, John," she said, each word taking some effort. Her belly was on fire, and staying conscious was like swimming upstream. She was very thirsty. "Kill that old bitch. I want to mount her ugly head over the bar in one of the saloons."

"I'll make a deal with you," Slocum said. "Get better and I'll hammer it in myself."

"Now that's a deal," Rose said, her chest rising and falling slowly.

Geezer and Doc Phipps came through the door, Doc Phipps was clutching his black bag. They crowded around her, and Doc Phipps pulled a stethoscope from his bag. He plugged it into his ears and ripped Rose's dress apart. He listened to her heartbeat. He'd heard better.

"She gonna make it, Doc?" Geezer asked.

Doc Phipps ignored him, trying not to look grim.

"We need to get her upstairs and into bed," he said. He looked around and spotted a pile of slightly mildewed tablecloths. "Those," Doc Phipps said. "Get me those tablecloths to keep her warm."

Slocum was reaching for the stack when Rose said, "Not the tablecloths. The bloodstains will never come out."

Under any other circumstances, Slocum would have smiled at that. He grabbed the tablecloths and covered Rose with them. Blood seeped through like water.

Doc Phipps turned to Geezer. "What are you waiting for? Go to my office and get the stretcher."

"Right, Doc," Geezer said, and disappeared up the steps.

"Give it to me straight, Doc," Rose said. "Will I ever play the violin again?"

"Try not to talk, Rose," Doc Phipps said, feeling the pulse in her neck.

"Try gettin' her not to," Slocum said.

Egbert and Donald Jones poked their heads through the door. Egbert called down, "Ma Fisher and one of her boys just lit out. Headin' south."

"You heard them, Slocum," Rose said, her voice faint. "Get off your butt and saddle up. We got an agreement."

Slocum gave her hand another squeeze.

"I'll be back," he said, and placed her hand gently on her chest. He leaned over and kissed her on the lips, then turned and climbed up the stairs. Halfway up, he wiped her blood from his mouth on his sleeve.

"Avenge me, John!" Rose cried from below with the last of her energy.

Slocum turned and looked down to her. Doc Phipps was tending to her the best he could.

"I'll do that," he said.

Now he was extremely angry.

13

Ma Fisher and Little Bo rode like the wind, south as the buzzard flies.

Her reputation would be seriously damaged as a result of the Roseville Massacre, as it would later come to be known. She'd started with almost a dozen men, including her idiot sons; now the feared Fisher gang was reduced to herself and Little Bo. The only way to keep her feared status in the outlaw community intact was to regroup below the border and then return to Roseville once more—and this time for keeps. Hell, she hadn't lasted all these years on luck alone.

She was too old, most likely, to spawn another brood, but any young'un who could be molded into her criminal needs would do. She envisioned an orgy of blood lust from one end of the West to the other. This time around, though, she'd round up a passel of the meanest, dumbest Meskin bandits she could find. Word was there were plenty to be had.

In the meantime, though, there was no point

thinking about the future when the present wasn't all peaches and cream. That smart bastard Slocum and his posse would be crawling up their asses if they didn't put some distance between them and Roseville. The question was how far the wily Slocum, who'd managed to mangle every one of her plans, would feel like giving chase. It was a long ride to Mexico, a week at least, and Slocum seemed like one of those single-minded, dedicated assholes who would chase her on one leg to China if he was of a mind to. He'd have to be dealt with.

"What now, Ma?" Little Bo shouted above the pounding hooves.

"I'm workin' on it," Ma shouted back, and rode faster.

Trying to organize a posse in Roseville was like trying to have a snowball fight in July.

The scene on Main Street was one of total havoc. Everyone knew there was a handsome bounty on Ma Fisher's head, and now that there was only Ma and Little Bo to deal with, the men of Roseville suddenly felt a lot braver. They ran every which way trying to round up their horses, all of whom had spooked during the shooting and were now scattered all over town. Charlie Russell's horse had crashed through the window of Cyrus Lawson's barbershop and was now chewing contentedly on the soap brushes. Across the street, Donald and Egbert Jones were chasing their half-blind, crippled father, who was hobbling on his cane and trying to get his hands on any horse he could.

"You cain't go, Pa," Egbert cried out as Norval Jones tried in vain to mount a horse, grabbing the stirrup and hopping up and down, one leg shy of mounting successfully.

"The hell I can't," Norval said, jumping high enough to fling himself up onto the saddle and toss aside his crutch. It hit Egbert square across the face and knocked him down. "This is the most fun I've had since your ma was in the mood," he cackled.

He spurred the left side of the horse and rode off, with Egbert and Donald running behind him.

"For Gawd's sake, Pa!" Donald yelled. "You cain't shoot what you cain't see!"

"Makes no difference," Norval cried. "I'm just goin' along for the ride. And so are y'all. Saddle up." Even with only one leg, Norval still looked at home sitting on a horse. "You're Joneses, so act like 'em."

Norval spurred the horse with everything he had. The horse, already nervous, reared up and sent Norval flying into a pile of cow patties, which barely cushioned the blow.

Donald and Egbert came running up, trying to catch him and missing by yards.

"Shit," he grunted, landing hard.

"That's right, Pa," Donald said as he and Egbert lifted their father to his foot, "and you're in it."

"Jumping butterballs," Norval ranted. "Get me back on that horse, you half-wits." He kicked his leg and slammed his fists into the dung.

Elsewhere, similar mayhem was unfolding. Men chased horses, while the horses chased stray cattle. The good men of Roseville tripped over themselves and everything else in an attempt to get to their horses. Slocum, with Geezer next to him, watched the spectacle with disgust.

"We got to get organized!" Slocum bellowed to the frantic would-be posse.

He fired two shots into the air to get their attention, and two more to make sure it stayed put. All eyes, man and animal alike, were on him.

"I'm leavin'!" Slocum yelled, and saddled up. "If you're comin', let's go." He slid his rifle into the scabbard and checked his six-shooter's chambers. He had enough ammunition to take on half the Sioux Nation if need be. "Just one thing before your trigger fingers get too itchy. Ma Fisher is mine, you understand? Anyone kills her before I do, well, just *don't*."

Nobody chose to argue.

Slocum put spurs to the horse's flanks and rode out. Geezer galloped out behind him, and one by one, the ranchers mounted and followed suit.

Ma wasn't particularly concerned about the posse that she knew from experience was hot on her trail. The men of Roseville were well-fed blowhards who didn't have the innards to give chase for long. She and her boy would easily outride them. No, it wasn't the posse that was worrying her.

It was that sidewinder who called himself Slocum.

And whoever was determined and crazy enough to follow him.

She'd shot it out with Pinkerton men, Texas Rangers, and federal marshals and had, by her gun, put close to fifty men, women, and children in their graves. She feared no one. Still, this Slocum was a man to reckon with. Sooner or later, she knew, she and Little Bo would have to make a stand.

"Look for a place where we can hole up," Ma called to her remaining son.

"Hole up?" Little Bo shrieked. "When there's a posse fixin' to slaughter us?"

"Shut up and do as I say," Ma barked. "I got me an idee."

"I had a snootful of your idees," Little Bo hollered back, trying to keep up with his mother. "Got all my brothers dead, 'cept for the one you killed. That weren't right, Ma."

"Sometimes the cards come up aces when fate deals 'em down, sometimes they come up jokers," Ma said. "The town looked like an easy touch. Far as Slug goes, the little bastard had it comin'."

Ma groaned as she pushed the horse even harder. The rheumatiz was kicking up again in her arms and legs and the burning in her belly—Ma Fisher had no idea what a peptic ulcer was, but that's just what she had—hurt worse than ever. Hard living and age were catching up with her, she knew. Even worse, the West was getting more and more civilized, making it damn tough for her kind to make a decent living. The outlaw days were numbered, Ma Fisher was painfully aware. Today's sickening spectacle testified to that. Time was, they'd have taken that town apart board by board and been halfway out of the territory by sundown looking for fresh blood. Now all of her boys were dead, and Slocum was responsible. She wanted to empty both barrels of her guns in his face and spit on his dead carcass, then watch the sun bleach his bones after the buzzards and the ants picked him clean.

That's just what she wanted.

•   •   •

Pretty much as Ma Fisher had predicted, many of Roseville's men quickly tired of the chase and wanted to head back.

Picking up Ma's trail had been easy, following it easier still. When dusk started to fall only a couple of hours after they'd taken pursuit, and their bellies started growling with hunger, their enthusiasm sank along with the sun.

The Jones brothers reined in their horses first, which caused the others to stop as well.

"What are we chasin' em for anyways?" Egbert said. "They ain't comin' back anytime soon."

"Yeah," Donald chimed in. "Let someone else worry about 'em. Ma Fisher ain't our problem now."

The seeds of doubt were planted and started to blossom. There were murmurs of agreement among the ranchers. This was no longer their fight. Geezer looked at Slocum for guidance.

"You're wrong," Slocum said. "She'll be back all right, if we let her get to Mexico so's she can regroup. She's got a score to settle with Roseville. We killed her sons, don't forget." Slocum spit into the dust. "Oh yes, she'll be back, and next time, she'll be in a *really* bad humor."

"That's your opinion, Slocum," Owen Grey piped up, "and we respect it. But that don't mean we agree with it. I got a ranch to tend to, and dead to bury as well. Egbert's right. Ma Fisher won't bother us again."

More murmurs of agreement were sounded. Slocum said, "Do whatever the hell you want. All I want to know is, who's with me?"

"Count me in," Geezer said. His words died on the wind. There were no other volunteers.

"So be it," Slocum said, and reined his horse back onto the Fishers' trail. "I'm sick of arguing with you lazy, knock-kneed *schlemiels*. Let's move, Geezer."

Geezer spat a stream of tobacco juice scornfully in the ranchers' direction and dutifully galloped off after Slocum.

"Don't seem right, Slocum fightin' all our battles," Egbert Jones said. "Think I had me a change of heart." He spurred his horse onward, and took off behind Slocum and Geezer.

"A lot of good it'll do you," Donald shouted. "You still have the same ugly face." But he, too, continued the hunt along with Slocum, Geezer, and his brother, against his better judgment. The rest of the posse turned tail and headed back to town.

Ma watched them come.

She was sequestered behind a rocky outcropping halfway up a ridge with her Winchester pointing straight at Slocum's chest as he and his three friends rode through the pass below. Little Bo was further on down the side of the stunted mountain, hidden by a clump of chinaberry trees and brush.

Ma Fisher waited until Slocum was securely in her gun sight before she squeezed the trigger of her Winchester. The pain of her rheumatiz had crept into her forefinger.

"So long, sucker," she hissed as the shot rang out. It went slightly wild, hitting his horse right in the side. The horse tumbled down and sent Slocum flying into the dirt.

Slocum hit the ground running, tearing the six-shooter from his gun belt and firing blindly in her general direction. Donald Jones was momentarily stunned, just long enough for his horse to spook and rear up on its hind legs. A second shot from Little Bo rang out and echoed, hitting Donald solid in the neck. He flopped to the ground, coughed twice, and died.

Slocum caught a faint glimpse of the gun smoke from the side of the hill. He crawled over to his dying horse and yanked the rifle from the scabbard. The bastards had bushwhacked him—and Slocum hated getting caught with his pants down. He hadn't expected Ma to try and ambush them this quickly. He cursed himself silently and fired off some shots in the direction of the gun smoke.

Geezer did the same. He'd already gotten down from his horse and was shooting. Egbert was panicking, screaming for his dead brother and for Jesus to help him. He tried frantically to turn his horse around, but before he could, he took a slug in the shoulder—courtesy of Ma's rifle. His entire body convulsed and he tumbled from his horse, flopping around in the dirt like a hooked catfish.

Slocum cocked his rifle and aimed at the rocks. Little Bo Fisher was dumb enough to stand up just long enough for Slocum to catch him in his sights. He fired and took Little Bo square in the chest. Little Bo dropped his rifle; it went clattering down against the rocks. He disappeared and didn't come back.

"Bastards!" they heard Ma Fisher bellow. Bullets barked and peppered the ground around Slocum, kicking up little puffs of dust.

Geezer and Slocum started blasting in the direction of Ma's anguished cries simultaneously. An eerie quiet fell over the pass when the shooting abruptly stopped. Egbert Jones was huddling behind a rock, whimpering like a newborn babe, his dead brother sprawled a few feet away.

"She's on the run," Geezer commented. "We got her now."

"I ain't so sure," was all Slocum said.

They were hidden behind a copse of walnut trees. Geezer took one tentative step out from behind the trees, then another. There was no return fire, so they cautiously made their way up the side of the ridge, fanning out on opposite sides. They were one hundred yards or so apart, separated by trees and hunks of rock.

Geezer found Little Bo wedged between two rocky outcroppings. His left leg was twisted hideously behind his back like a length of barbed wire. His head had borne the brunt of his fall, and was smashed all to hell with his brains showing. Above him, buzzards were already circling hungrily.

"Definitely like you better dead," Geezer said to Little Bo's corpse, but out of respect, he picked up the kid's hat, which had landed five feet away, and placed it over Little Bo's pulpy face.

Geezer started back up the slope. Ma stepped out from a clump of brush, six-guns in each hand, and fired each twice. Burning lead ripped through Geezer's back and legs. He plummeted forward and hit the ground hard, after bouncing off a tree.

Ma went over to him and prodded his body with the point of her boot, and Geezer flopped onto his back. He was still breathing. His eyes were fluttering weakly. He opened them only to see Ma Fisher's ugly face peering down at him. A stream of tobacco juice squirted from the corner of his mouth.

"Old Geezer, I shoulda knowed," she drawled.

"Ya know, your biscuits tasted like shit."

"So I been told," Geezer rasped.

"Coffee tasted like gopher piss, too," she said, pointing the .45 at his head and cocking the trigger. "Say your prayers, old man," she hissed.

"No, say yours, bitch," Slocum hissed from behind her, and barely waited for her to turn before he squeezed off three shots that took her in the side, the calf of her left leg, and the third took a nice chunk out of her shoulder. Still, Ma managed to squeeze off two shots that pinged harmlessly into the dirt a yard away from him before she fell to the ground, one six-gun flew from her left hand. Before she even hit the dirt Slocum was on her, and kicked the other gun out of her hand. Flat on her back now, she reached out almost instinctively with her free hand and tried to get the gun she'd dropped. Slocum slammed his foot down on her wrist and heard it snap. Ma wailed in pain. It was music to Slocum's ears.

"You caused me a lot of grief," Slocum said to her. He pointed his pistol in her face. "Give me one good reason why I shouldn't blow your ugly head off now."

Blood oozed from her wounds. She said, "You wouldn't kill a woman, would ya?"

Slocum cocked the trigger and pointed the gun closer to her head. Ma shut her eyes, and Slocum saw true fear on her face. For one brief moment he saw a human being; someone who under different circumstances might have been a decent wife and mother, hanging out the wash instead of slaughtering innocent people. Someone, given half a chance, that might have been a productive member of society.

Hell, she was about the same age as his mother would have been.

Slocum swallowed hard, then slowly holstered his pistol. A look of sour triumph passed over Ma's face. Slocum turned and started to walk away. He took a few steps in Geezer's direction but watched her like a hawk. He stopped abruptly.

"Fuck it," he murmured. He turned back, drew his gun, and fired a couple of shots into Ma's heart. She had just enough time, barely half a second, for her face to register shock, before her chest exploded like a pink piglet that was fed a stick of dynamite. Her body jerked violently. Her face, in death, was etched in a white mask of agony, with her eyes still open wide. Only when one of her legs twitched twice then lay still was Slocum convinced that she was dead for sure.

"You ain't nearly as nice as my ma was," Slocum muttered.

He walked over to Geezer, who was struggling, futilely, to get up. Each movement, Slocum could see, was a new adventure in pain.

Slocum knelt down beside him.

Geezer said weakly, "Got me in the liver, she did."

"Don't worry," Slocum said. "Can't kill something twice."

"She dead?"

Slocum said, "She is indeed."

"I'm relieved," Geezer said, and then died.

Slocum gently closed Geezer's lifeless eyes with his fingers.

"Owe you one, partner," he said.

He hoisted Geezer's lifeless body onto his back

and made his way to where Egbert Jones and the horses were waiting. He'd see to it personally that Geezer got a proper Christian burial.

Down below, Egbert was mourning his dead brother as Slocum heaved Geezer over the saddle of his horse. He yelled for Egbert to dry his tears and do the same with his deceased brother. Egbert's wound wasn't too bad. He'd live.

"Let's be goin'," Slocum said, and suddenly remembered something Rose had said earlier that day.

Something, he now recalled, about wanting to mount Ma Fisher's head over the bar of one of her saloons.

Slocum thought about it. Then he thought about it some more.

"You get them?" Rose asked weakly.

She was lying in a bed in one of the second-floor rooms. Doc Phipps, looking grave, his shirt covered with her blood, wiped her brow with a cloth. Her face was whiter than six-month-old cheese; talking, even swallowing, was a supreme effort.

"Buzzards ought to be pickin' their teeth right about now," Slocum said.

"Got the slugs out," Doc Phipps whispered to Slocum, "fer what that's worth."

Slocum whispered back, "She going to make it?"

Doc Phipps murmured, "Never seen anything like it. Taken bullets out of half the infantrymen at Shiloh, and even the toughest of 'em passed on with wounds like hers. Never seen a person hang onto life like her. Don't want to leave this earth without sayin' goodbye to you, I suspect."

Slocum swallowed hard and knelt down at Rose's

bedside. He took her hand in his. It was cold to his touch.

"Doc says you're going to be all right," Slocum said, a solid lump rising in his throat. Deep in his guts he felt something powerful for this woman.

"You're cute when you lie," Rose rasped.

Slocum kissed her hand, because he wanted to.

"If I didn't have all these holes in me," she said, "I'd give you a tumble."

"I'll settle for some heavy breathing—yours," he said.

"How about a kiss?" she said even weaker than before, her voice sounding smaller than a baby ant.

Slocum leaned over and kissed her gently on the lips. With this, she smiled a little, then closed her eyes and went to sleep. Doc Phipps moved in quickly and put the cold cup of his stethoscope to her chest. Her breathing was erratic, but it was better than none at all.

"It's anybody's guess whether she'll make it another hour," Doc Phipps said. "She may surprise us all, but the odds are against it."

Slocum couldn't seem to release her hand, clutching it tightly as though willing part of his spirit, his life, to flow into her, and keep her alive. His head full of cobwebs, he barely heard Doc Phipps say to him, "Go downstairs and get yourself some whiskey, John. She's in the hands of the Lord now." He gently ushered Slocum out of the room.

"She's fixin' to die, ain't she?" Slocum asked.

Doc Phipps looked like he wanted to cry. "Don't bet against it."

Slocum went sluggishly to the bar. By this time, things in town had almost returned to normal. Solly saw Slocum coming and placed a glass and a bottle on the bar. He took the liberty of pouring Slocum a shot.

There were a couple of people standing at the bar, plus a few seated at tables. Ranch hands, most of them. They looked exhausted, more from tension than from a lack of sleep. Almost battle weary, Slocum thought.

He threw back the contents of the shot glass. Solly poured him another. Slocum downed it just as quickly.

"We're grateful for all your help, Mister Slocum," Solly said. He poured Slocum another. "On the house."

"Yeah," Slocum sipped his whiskey slowly this time, thoughtfully. He looked up from his drink, took a small sip, and said to Solly, "That work of art behind your bar looks a little crooked. Two inches, I'd say."

Solly turned with the bottle still clenched in his fist, and looked up at the framed mural directly above the bar. He grabbed a stool, stepped on it, and attempted to make the newest work of art, Ma Fisher's head, which Slocum had neatly mounted on a board of oak—not hang unevenly. He skillfully righted the trophy.

Slocum knew that Ma's head would last at least a week mounted above the bar before disintegrating into a gray clump of rotten flesh. He wanted to see Ma Fisher's skinless skull hanging over this very bar, after the brittle flesh on her hideous face turned into dust and mixed with the sawdust on the floor.

Solly stepped down from the stool, having straightened Slocum's contribution to modern art, and sloshed more hooch into Slocum's glass. Slocum sipped this one slowly as well.

"Anything else I can get for you, Mister Slocum?" Solly asked. "Some food, maybe?"

Slocum took his time downing this drink. He slammed the shot glass down onto the bar, then wiped his mouth on his sleeve.

"No thanks," he said. "I'll get over it. I always do."

Solly poured him another drink, then poured one for himself.

He raised his glass. "To Miss Rose."

Slocum nodded and raised his glass. They downed their shots to befit the toast.

Slocum said, "I'll drink to that."

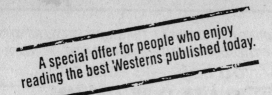

A special offer for people who enjoy reading the best Westerns published today.

WESTERNS!

NO OBLIGATION

Mail the coupon below

To start your subscription and receive 2 FREE WESTERNS, fill out the coupon below and mail it today. We'll send your first shipment which includes 2 FREE BOOKS as soon as we receive it.

- -

Mail To: **True Value Home Subscription Services, Inc. P.O. Box 5235**
120 Brighton Road, Clifton, New Jersey 07015-5235

YES! I want to start reviewing the very best Westerns being published today. Send me my first shipment of 6 Westerns for me to preview FREE for 10 days. If I decide to keep them, I'll pay for just 4 of the books at the low subscriber price of $2.75 each: a total $11.00 (a $21.00 value). Then each month I'll receive the 6 newest and best Westerns to preview Free for 10 days. If I'm not satisfied I may return them within 10 days and owe nothing. Otherwise I'll be billed at the special low subscriber rate of $2.75 each; a total of $16.50 (at least a $21.00 value) and save $4.50 off the publishers price. There are never any shipping, handling or other hidden charges. I understand I am under no obligation to purchase any number of books and I can cancel my subscription at any time, no questions asked. In any case the 2 FREE books are mine to keep.

Name _____

Street Address _____ Apt. No. _____

City _____ State _____ Zip Code _____

Telephone _____

Signature _____
(if under 18 parent or guardian must sign)

Terms and prices subject to change. Orders subject
to acceptance by True Value Home Subscription
Services, Inc.

14010-5